I0741898

AFTERLIFE LOVE STREAMS

Other Books by Mark Jay Mann

Collection of Wordstreams
Homeless Mysteries, Homeless Intimacies
Astrology for the Absolute Beginner

AFTERLIFE LOVESTREAMS

Journeys Through Caregiving, Grieving and Into Beyond Life Dimensions to Reconnect With My Lost Love

MARK JAY MANN

The painting of Dancing Girls in Orphanage was part of a collection of art pieces Diana Zelaya created based on her life in an orphanage from age three to nine. This painting reflects the joy she often felt dancing with the other children on the orphanage grounds as music was playing on a loudspeaker. Diana is the girl in the red dress dancing alone. You will find Diana's art interspersed throughout this book along with a special focus on her works in Appendix I.

Published by:
Breakthrough Enterprises
P.O. Box 5511
Eugene, OR 97405

ISBN: 978-0-9648470-4-0

*This book is dedicated to Diana, my love and partner
in life and in the afterlife*

Acknowledgments

I want to acknowledge Doug Hoss, who provided invaluable editing and design services, and who formatted both the eBook and print versions, including the cover.

I also want to thank Marjorie Beck of Flawless Documents, who also provided editing and proofreading services.

Tracy Murfitt, our oldest daughter, was so helpful in providing feedback during the various revisions of this book.

Robert Gulley also assisted in the final stages of proofreading, and also provided the photograph of the Moon Gate and gave me permission to use it.

I want to thank Katy Keuter, our third oldest daughter, and her daughter, Iris Keuter, who provided additional formatting and design assistance.

I want to acknowledge Dr. Terri Daniel, who founded the Afterlife Conference in 2010, which each year has a goal of uniting "the disciplines in exploring the survival of the consciousness after death, working with hospice professionals, physicians, mediums, clergy, counselors, and alternative healers to offer a deeper understanding of death and beyond." I was able to attend the 2019 conference, and found it inspiring and helpful in my own grieving process. There were many professional and informative workshop presenters and speakers at the conference, such as Suzanne Northrop, Austyn Wells, Janet Piedilato, Linda Fitch, Linda Backman, Phil Borges and Dr. Brian Richards. For more information about the conference and Dr. Daniel's books, classes and other services, see her websites at:

http://afterlifeconference.com and

https://www.danieldirect.net/terri-daniel-.html

Table of Contents

Prologue

My wife passed away on March 24, 2018. We had been together for 41 years, and I had been caring for her for the previous 5 years when she was diagnosed with Alzheimer's disease. As she passed, I made a promise to her that I would find her in the afterlife dimensions. This book covers the weeks before she passed and my grieving and adjustments during the weeks after she passed. This book is also the result of my own journeys into beyond life dimensions using what I refer to as my spiritual imagination. As the story unfolds, I hope it inspires transformative and entertaining experiences, reflections, and insights within each reader's own spiritual imagination, especially related to finding peaceful acceptance and excitement of our own eventual passing into the afterlife… into beyond life dimensions.

The reader will notice that I use the terms *afterlife* as well as *beyond life dimensions.* I use the term *afterlife* to refer to the time after the consciousness of an individual's transition from their bodies in the earth realm into beyond life dimensions. I use the term *beyond life dimensions* to refer to spiritual realities that I believe exist beyond the limits of time cycles and longitude-latitude space. These time-space factors in the earth realm structure and give meaning to our lives while we exist in human physical form.

Beyond life dimensions are what we transition into as we enter the afterlife, but I believe these dimensions can be entered into and accessed while we are living within our earth body consciousness. We enter into these dimensions unconsciously through our dreams and reveries, but we can also develop the inner capacities to enter into these realms consciously with spiritual and imaginative intent. While few have chosen to develop these conscious inner capacities in an objective, compassionate, and inclusive manner, more and more individuals are choosing to do so. And by doing so, these individuals can not only experience the wonderment, magic, empathetic love, and ethereal beauty in the beyond life dimensions, but can share the wisdom gained with others to enhance life in the earth realm. As more and more individuals access these beyond life dimensions consciously, I believe the evolution of positive human existence living in the earth realm will be enhanced.

Diana was one of the individuals who was consciously and unconsciously open to beyond life dimensions. Her earthbound wisdom allowed her to enhance the lives of her children, extended family, and friends with the spiritual and imaginative qualities she had gained.

Music to Accompany This Reading Experience:

As you read this book, you will notice the importance that music has been to Diana's and my shared life together, to my grieving process as I healed and adjusted to her leaving this earth realm, and as I developed my abilities to journey into afterlife dimensions. As I wrote this book, I listened to playlists of specific music that both comforted and inspired me. As I finished the book, I fantasized that the reader's experience could be enhanced by also listening to the same music I was listening to as I was writing. If readers want to do this, they may have their own music that they would prefer to listen to, but in Appendix II I've listed music that I listened to as wrote this book.

Part I

My Promise to Diana As She Passed

My Promise to My Love as She Left the Earth Realm

My hand lay softly on her chest. Even though her eyes had not been open for days, I still could feel the beating of her heart, the gentle rhythm of her breathing, her presence lingering in this realm.

My head had been bent forward, resting on the pillow next to her, my eyes also closed, but then I looked up as I felt motion in the space around us. Perhaps her soul, still connected to this realm, was swirling around, ready to flow away. I gazed at her face, her glowing and vibrant brown skin tone, surrounded by her still black and thick hair at age 76, and the pink fake flower that one of our grandchildren had clipped to the side of her hair. Various friends and family who came to visit often thought the pink rose in her hair was real and were amazed how long it remained alive.

Diana lay under a bright red knitted bedspread. Two candles, incense, and an arrangement of flowers, white orchids, sat on a tall table that served as headboard between the hospice bed and the east window. The time was nearing 5:00pm, but the spring equinox had occurred a few days earlier, and the afternoon light filtered through the thin India cotton curtains covering the three tall windows in the room, adding to the serene atmosphere.

Our close friend Antonia Putzi Esmario, who is a shaman, sat beside me near my dying wife. Antonia said she could see Diana's soul flowing back and forth on a golden stream of light that extended from her heart to somewhere beyond this earth realm, but she said the essence of my wife kept flowing back into her psyche, back into her body.

"She does not want to leave you," Antonia said, "And she is concerned about you—that you will be ok."

I looked at my wife and focused on opening my whole being to her soul. I said to her, *Go on your journey, my love, and know that I will be OK while I am still here in this realm. I will try to connect with you while I am still here through dreams, through meditating, through listening to the music that we love, though using whatever spiritual rituals I need to. But also know that I will follow you when it is my time to die. I will seek to connect with you, with your essence wherever you are existing, I promise with all my heart and soul. I will find you again—even while I am in this body. I will find a way to journey into the spirit world to connect with you. I promise.*

I held her hand, leaned over and kissed her lips and her cheeks.

Then our shaman friend placed one of her hands over Diana's heart. "She will be going now," Antonia said. "She heard you and she will be waiting for you."

I then felt the rhythm of her faint breathing stop. The essence of her soul had passed.

Antonia left shortly after. I stood up and walked to the foot of Diana's bed. I gazed around the room that had been decorated by my wife's artistry and craft skills. Curtains and pillows she had sewn, painting and photographs she had framed, the bulletin board sitting on a dark wood cabinet full of recent photographs of our children, grandchildren, friends. I looked closely at one photograph pinned to the board, of my wife in her mid-twenties.

I took my phone out and as "La Soledad," one of our favorite Pink Martini songs played, I began videoing from my position in the center of the room, starting with her under the covers of a bright red knitted blanket, then circling slowing around the room hovering on my wife's various art and decorations, then just as the music was ending, I focused on the bulletin board of photos and came to rest on the photo of my wife in her twenties and then turned back to her as she lay peacefully in her bed.

"Go where you need to go, my love. I will find you wherever you go, wherever you are. I promise."

Part II

Who Was Diana Zelaya in Her Recent Life on Earth?

Excerpts from Diana Zelaya's Obituary
(Full obituary on legacy.com)

March 12, 1942 –
March 24, 2018

Diana Zelaya transitioned away peacefully in the comfort of her home with her life-love partner and family members near her on March 24, 2018 at 5:10 pm. She had been living with Alzheimer's for at least 5 years.

Diana was a mother to 6 children (4 daughters, 1 son and 1 stepson), ages 48 to 54 at the time of her passing. She was an Oma to 13 grandchildren, ages 8 to 27 at the time of her passing.

Diana was born in Chicago, and has Spanish ancestry (though her mother was from Nicaragua and father was from Mexico). Diana was in a Catholic orphanage cared for by German Nuns from age 3-9, and then eventually her single mother was able to bring her and her siblings back to live with her. Diana loved her time in the orphanage. She said she felt comfortable and secure in the orphanage's walled grounds that were isolated from the rest of the city and with the orderliness of the daily routines.

One of Diana's favorite activities when she was in high school was reading National Geographic and other articles or books about Europe and other parts of the world. She had wanted to join the Peace Corps when she graduated from high school. Instead, she chose to marry Jim Derby and over the next years gave birth to their 5 children. After she had her last child, she told her husband she wanted to live in Europe. They agreed that he would stay working for a while and then join her in Europe. Diana took the children by herself to Bavaria with very little money. It was quite a special journey for her, with women strangers helping her and her children in New York and Paris and providing places for them to stay. She eventually arrived in a small town outside Munich (Rosenheim). They lived in Bavaria for a year and made close German friends, who remained her closest friends throughout her life.

When she and her family moved back to the United States in 1973, they first settled in Boise, Idaho, but in 1975 they chose to move to Eugene, Oregon, because the creative and progressive environment resonated more with them. Diana separated from her husband in 1976 and began living with Mark in 1977.

During the rest of her life, Diana traveled extensively in Europe, mostly with Mark, but occasionally by herself. She had always wanted to live in Europe, but loved the access to organic foods and progressive atmosphere in Eugene, and as the grandchildren were born, she wanted to remain in Eugene to share with her children and grandchildren. However, every few years she traveled to Europe. Their favorite places in Europe were Prague, Paris, Istanbul, Florence, and Southern Portugal.

In 1980, Diana completed a B.A. in Fine Arts at the University of Oregon. She was highly skilled in pen and ink drawings, watercolors, and oil painting. One of her specialties was portrait paintings. She completed three charcoal drawings and a painting of memories of her time in the orphanage.

In 1989, Diana completed a Master's Degree in Social Work at Portland State University. She had a Jungian-oriented therapy practice with adults, couples, and specializing in counseling children. In the early 1980s, she went through a few years of Jungian analysis. Her psychologist used the analysis of some of her extensive number of dreams as part of her Jungian thesis, which is currently in the library at the Jungian Institute in Switzerland. In 1985 Diana was invited to attend the Jungian Summer Program in Küsnacht, Switzerland. In her practice she used sand tray therapy as one of her interventions both with children and adults. In 1991, she volunteered for 4 months to care for orphans in Romania.

She was highly knowledgeable in alternative healing, and since the 1970s raised her children with natural and organic foods, cooking meals from scratch. In the years before her illness, she had a particular interest in Ayurveda healing and cooking.

Diana has always been connected to spiritual pursuits. Sharing thoughts and experiences about holistic and inclusive psychological and spiritual pursuits were important in her relationship with Mark. Diana loved listening to a wide variety of music, but during the last few years enjoyed Luciano Pavarotti, Andrea Bocelli, and Pink Martini. Her favorite songs include My Sweet Lord (George Harrison), Heaven (Joe Cocker), Layla (Eric Clapton), and a variety of music from around the world. During her years with Alzheimer's she was still able to remember lyrics and sing along while listening to her favorite songs. She also listened to a variety of spiritual music and chants.

Diana had a high level of writing skills. She used to know a little German, Spanish, French, Italian and Latin, and seemed to understand these languages when spoken even during these last years. She studied Latin all through her Catholic schooling, and this language knowledge seemed to enhance her vocabulary. She helped Mark edit three books he has published.

Diana designed the Mediterranean style house that she

and Mark have lived in, and completely decorated the interiors and exteriors and designed the landscape. She was an avid gardener. She was a skilled seamstress and made all of her daughters' prom and wedding dresses, as well as most of the curtains, cloth hangings, and pillows in their house.

Diana and Mark joined the Tiara Intentional Neighborhood in 1995, and built their house in this community. This community was built on the values of interactive sharing and engagement, environmental sustainability, global inclusiveness, and progressive, community engagement. The close connections and interactions with their neighbors have been a sustaining and supportive part of their lives.

Diana was well-grounded, but had a highly intuitive and empathetic nature. She gave family, friends and acquaintances unconditional respect and love, while also being able to set her limits and be direct and honest in a caring but firm manner when necessary.

Volunteer to assess Romanian orphans

By KIMBER WILLIAMS
The Register-Guard

As a Eugene social worker, Diana Zelaya has spent ample time assessing the needs of young children. Now she'd like to apply that skill in a new way.

For the next three months, Zelaya will serve as a volunteer with the Free Romania Foundation Inc., a Massachusetts-based agency that attempts to help the country's orphans.

Founded by Ion Berindei, a Romanian architect who left his homeland 20 years ago, the program uses professionals and volunteers to work with children in orphanages, foster homes and rehabilitation programs.

Zelaya will be assisting with the Touch Program, one of several projects designed to help Romania's disabled orphans. "The volunteers will help identify children who could benefit from being adopted although

Volunteers are trained to administer developmental screening tests and simple medical evaluations, such as weighing and measuring the children.

"A lot of these children are misdiagnosed. Evaluations are very haphazard and done by ill-qualified people. We are trying to change the attitudes of staff workers by providing positive examples, rewarding those who really care as opposed to those who totally ignore the possibility for improvement," Berindei said.

The foundation has sent about 70 volunteers to Romania since January. The Cambridge-based organization has registered chapter offices in New York, Connecticut, California, Atlanta and Dallas.

As a volunteer, Zelaya must pay $3,000 to participate in the program. Part of the amount covers her own transportation costs, lodging and personal expenses while in Romania. The remainder supports the non-profit foundation.

An article about Diana Zelaya in the April 24th, 1991 edition of the Eugene Register-Guard newspaper

Volunteering at a Romanian Orphanage in 1991

A few years after Diana completed her Master of Social Work Degree at Portland State University, she chose to serve as a volunteer for the Free Romania Foundation's Touch Program. One of the goals of this program was to help identify the care needed to rehabilitate disabled children who had not been provided the proper caregiving and medical attention under the authoritarian Romanian President, Nicolae Ceausescu. Another goal was to assist in preparing disabled orphans for adoption.

Diana was to serve as a volunteer for three months in a rural orphanage in northern Romania near the Black Sea. She provided developmental screening and basic evaluations of the physical conditions of the children. Under the Ceausescu government, orphans were kept in terrible conditions—forced to sleep in cribs, even as they became teenagers, and often on soiled mattresses. They were malnourished and not provided sufficient opportunities for physical exercise or behavior guidance.

Diana found many of the rural people she met caring and appreciative. Along with the other volunteers, she found interacting with the children rewarding. She felt that significant, life-changing progress was being made in helping the children receive the proper care and, in many cases, be adopted.

The one problem that Diana struggled with was the environmental conditions that had deteriorated under the communist Ceausescu government. Much of the water was contaminated with gasoline, and the air quality was unhealthy. A few weeks before the end of her three months stay, Diana became ill with a respiratory condition, and she and another volunteer who had also become ill had to leave early. They hired a local driver to take them to Munich, Germany, where Diana stayed with friends while she received medical care from a German Naturopathic physician as she healed. Despite her temporary illness, Diana felt gratified that she could be a part of the volunteer services that allowed these children to receive proper medical care and opportunities to be adopted into loving families.

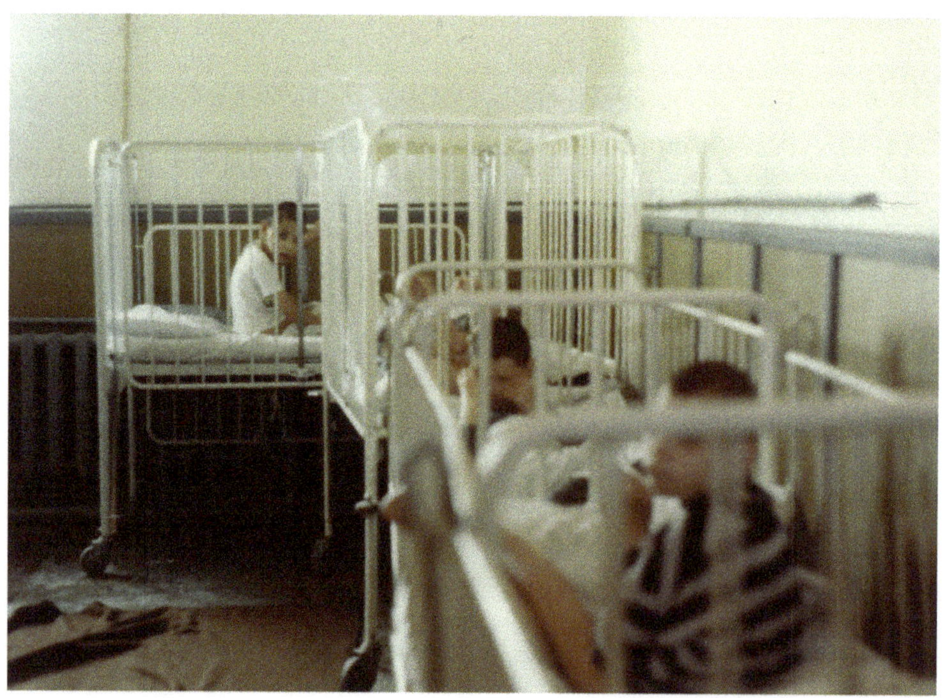

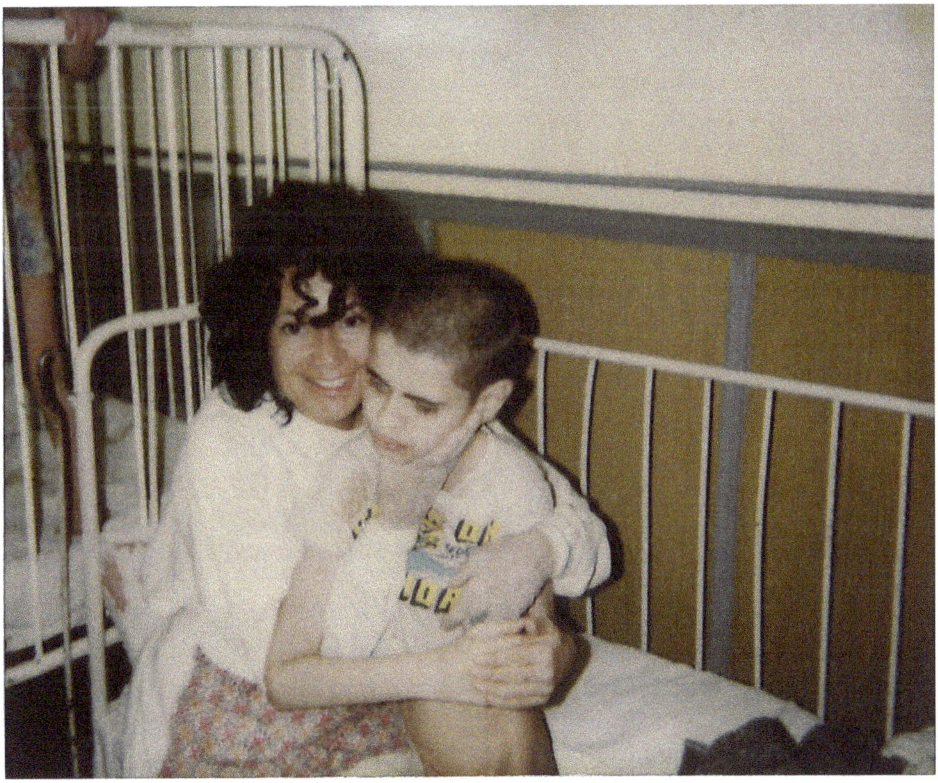

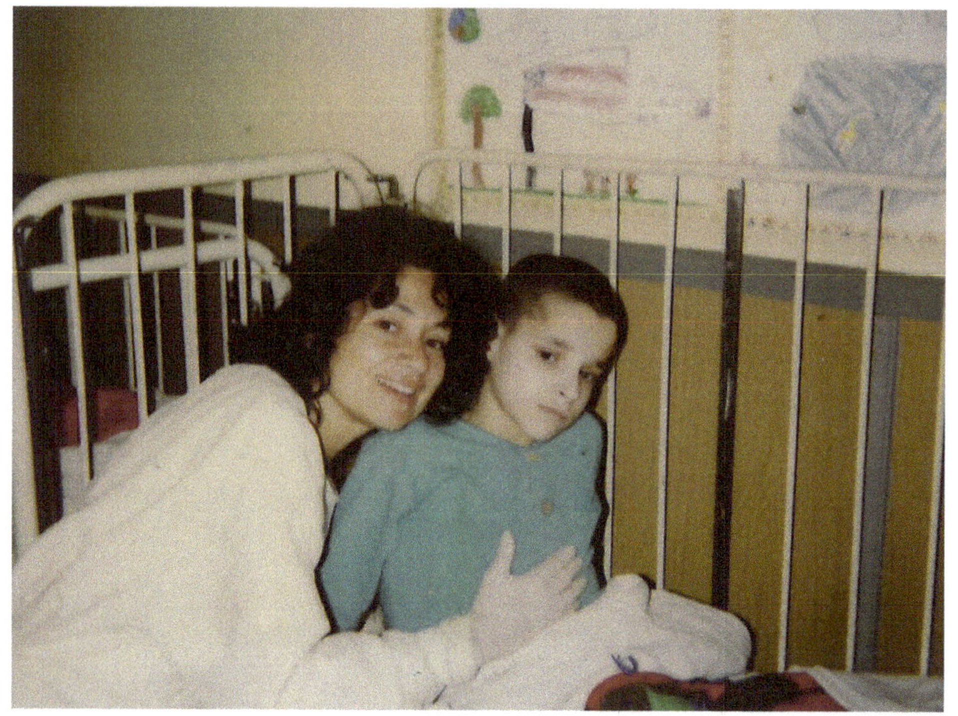

The Spiritual Mediterranean-style House That Diana Designed

Diana designed our Mediterranean-style house that surrounds an inner courtyard on three sides with a wall with a window made of a metal grille facing the street to complete the enclosure. The main parts of the house are on the west and north sides. The smaller guest house sits on the east.

We lived for 15 years in the main part of the house, but right before Diana was diagnosed with Alzheimer's she said she wanted to move into the smaller guest house. She said she wanted to live in a smaller space where we could handle the cleaning and upkeep easier. Maybe she intuitively knew that her consciousness would be expanding beyond the rational mind and her perceptions would be focused more on the spirit world than on the day to day organization and order of the earth realm. Diana was capable of creating such aesthetic and comfortable environments in the places we lived, and she did the same as we moved into the smaller guest house.

DESIGN
DIANA ZELAYA
CONSTRUCTION
STEPHEN PASAVATZ
WAYNE PREVITI
DRAWINGS
ANTJE FRAXLER
EAST ELEVATION
SOUTH ELEVATION

The building material used for the outside walls was a po-
rous material called Rastra (8 inches thick) made of concrete and recycled polystyrene. This material allowed her
to carve ornamental designs over many of the windows.

The courtyard had three wooden, dark brown stained Tuscan tapered columns we had found in a used building materials store in Portland, and she had the builder connect them with arches. They sat on a lower stone wall that separates the loggia from the rest of the courtyard.

She had built a wooden black stained picket fence along part of the sides of the house to keep the deer from eating the flowers and plants. There were three wooden gates; each had a different symbol carved in the wood. One was the Sun Gate, one was the Moon Gate, and the other was the Star Gate. She arranged to have a local artist and metal worker build a simple, yet artistic iron gate leading to the entrance of the house.

Moon Gate

Star Gate

Ethan Derby

Ava Derby

Diana watering garden in front of Sun Gate

After this house was built and we moved in, I have always felt this was Diana's artistic masterpiece. The house and the garden she also created reflects the blend of her earthy, exotic, and spiritual attunement.

Our Children and Grandchildren

During the years of Diana's Alzheimer's, she would often stand in front of this bulletin board for long periods of time, looking at these photographs of the kids and grandkids. Then as her condition progressed, she would talk to various of the kids as if they were present. She would laugh as she talked and asked them why they weren't responding to her. She would say things like, "I hope you will tell me how you are doing," and in a lower, whispering voice, "Maybe you will even tell me your secrets, and I promise I won't tell anyone. I love your smiles. You seem so happy."

The kids would often send her videos of themselves saying hello to Oma and talking a little bit about themselves. I put these videos on a DVD and would play it for her. Each time she was delighted to hear them, and again would try to talk with them, and would wave goodbye as each video ended. She would look at these videos often, and each time it would be like she had never seen them before, as she felt the same joy and excitement with her kids and grandkids communicating with her as if they were actually present. And they were, in her imagination.

When I began living with Diana and her children, I realized that she was consistent, not just with her unconditional love and nurturing guidance, but also with her insistence that they be considerate and respectful of others in their interactions. She also had begun requiring the children to do a few chores to help out around the house. I remember her creating colorful chore reminders that the kids could easily follow:

	INSPECTOR	SWEEPER	TABLE	GARBAGE
	KATY	ALICIA	JIM	MADELINE
	MADELINE	KATY	ALICIA	JIM
AUG 7	JIM	MADELINE	KATY	ALICIA
AUG 14	ALICIA	JIM	MADELINE	KATY
AUG 21	KATY	ALICIA	JIM	MADELINE
AUG 28	MADELINE	KATY	ALICIA	JIM
SEPT 4	JIM	MADELINE	KATY	ALICIA
SEPT 11	ALICIA	JIM	MADELINE	KATY
SEPT 18	KATY	ALICIA	JIM	MADELINE
SEPT 25	MADELINE	KATY	ALICIA	JIM
	...REMIND OTHERS OF THEIR JOBS IN THE MOST PLEASANT WAY...	...CLEARS DINNER DISHES, AND SWEEPS AFTER DINNER MEAL..	...SETS BREAKFAST LUNCH AND DINNER DISHES..	..CHECKS EVERY DAY - EMPTYS WHEN NECESSARY - REMINDS MARK OR DAD TO GO TO DUMP...

When she started this chore list, each of the youngest four children were ages 6 to 12 (Tracy, our oldest, was assigned other duties). Each child was asked to do one of four tasks for a week and then rotate to another task for the next week and so on. Each month each of our youngest children would share in doing all four tasks. Three of the tasks were very straightforward: Sweeper (Clears dinner dishes and sweeps after dinner meal); Table (sets breakfast, lunch and clears dishes); Garbage (Checks every day—empty when necessary). I found that the final task was amazing. She titled it the Inspector. She described the task in this way: "Remind others of their jobs in the most pleasant way...."

From middle school through high school, the children were required to do their own laundry and ironing, and each had to cook for the family one night each week. Until the children graduated high school, they were required to be home for family dinners each school night, except for special occasions. Diana was insistent that the children would not bring into the house regular soda pop (at that time very few natural sodas were on the market).

As the children entered high school, they were allowed a great deal of independence and encouragement to pursue their own activities and interests. I have to say that Diana taught me so much about the balances of love and discipline, of freedom and responsibility, of family sharing and encouraging independence in child rearing dynamics. We worked well together as we raised our children.

I came across a photograph that had been taken when

the children were very young in Bavaria. It seems to reflect how Diana encouraged her children to each express their uniqueness in expressive and colorful ways:

The Moment of Birth of an Old Soul

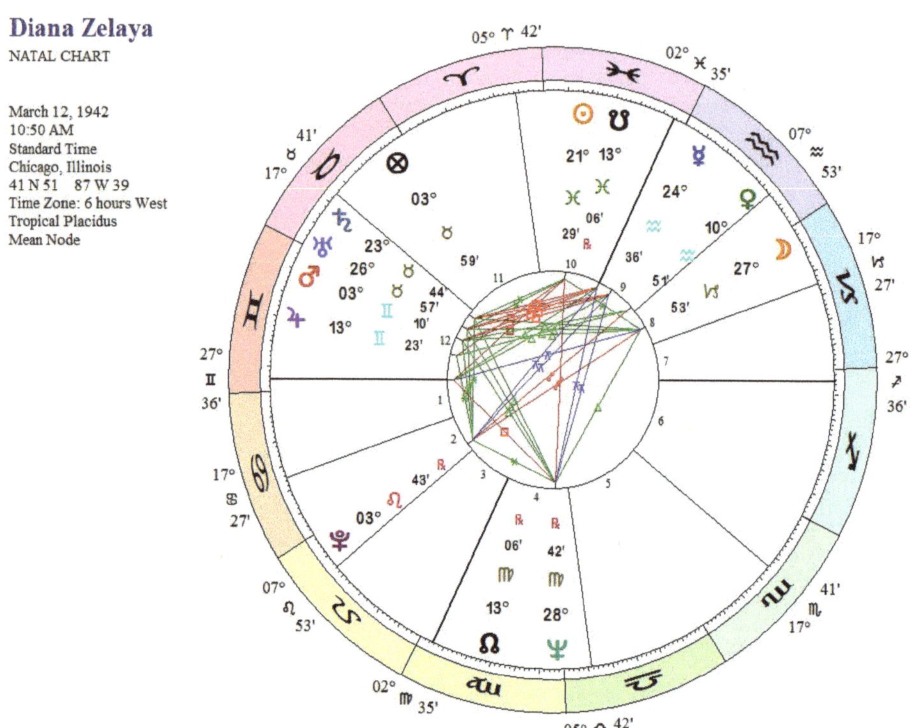

Even if you do not know anything about astrology, I ask you to notice the kite formation of the major planets' positions in the tropical zodiac the moment Diana was born related to her birthplace on earth. The top of the kite is where her Sun was located in Pisces, indicating a natural attunement to spiritual dimensions—artistic and highly imaginative endeavors, a rich dream world, empathic and compassionate. The lower triangle of planets show a flowing relationship with each in earth signs (Capricorn, Taurus, and Virgo). This means that one of Diana's purposes in this life is to bring spiritual and imaginative attunements that perhaps she has developed over lifetimes on earth and in other dimensions—to bring these

developed spiritual attunements down to earth and enhance the material and physical nature of the world with
beauty that combines the exotic with the mundane. The
bottom of the kite is centered in the area that relates to
home and family. She had a natural ability to be consistent with her discipline and nurturing as she raised her
children and gave counseling guidance to other families
and children.

The Golden Kite

Reflections on Diana's birth chart pattern

Your soul is like a golden kite,
an eternal design, strong yet light,
floating through the universe
in an elegant and inspiring flight.

Your soul is like a golden kite,
with the higher, smaller triangle
pointing upward beyond the skies,
supported by the lower larger triangle
pointing downward toward the earth,
where it remains connected
despite how far away you fly
by the shimmering filament threads
woven with wisdom gained from the lives you've led.

Your soul is like a golden kite,
made of ancient artful lines,
shaped into sextiles and trines
symbolizing your flowing sensitivities
and your spirituality that has integrated
earth, water, and air,
while exploring fiery stars
in dimensions near and far.

You have flown often to unknown places,
on the winds of dreams and visions within,
then come back time and time again
bringing your treasures
of compassion, nurturance, and beauty,
to share with family and friends alike.
Your soul is like a golden kite.

Part III

The Weeks Before She Passed— Caregiving & Preparing

Caregiving for you, my love, as you progress through your illness, is allowing us to blend our two separate beings even more completely, through moment to moment depths of sharing of our human vulnerabilities and spiritual strengths. Caregiving for you is the ultimate gift of intimacy that you are giving me.

Morning Light and Shadows

This morning when I woke up to see how Diana was doing, I was standing by the kitchen sink looking out the window at the after-dawn sunlight casting shadows on the white stucco wall in the courtyard—thin shadows of rose vines, tree limbs, the hanging outdoor metal chandelier intertwined gracefully.

The sky was clear above—and I felt invigorated by the natural flow of light in this early March day. The last few weeks or longer have been so overcast. I gave thanks to the passage of time that can bring such renewals—the coming spring light reflecting in my psyche—new hopes—as well as a deeply felt appreciation of each moment providing me the opportunity to enjoy the love of my life while she remained alive in this time-space realm.

I looked over at Diana lying in the hospice bed in the front room. She was still sleeping. The eastern sun rising outside the window behind her bed shone through the thin white India cotton curtain and cast a warm light around Diana.

She is so precious. I cherish each moment I have with her.

I decided to let her sleep a little longer, but I knew I would have to get her up soon for breakfast.

Each Precious Moment with You

Diana may pass within weeks. Another jolt of reality occurred today with the visit of our hospice nurse. She was very informative, thoughtful. She spent time, did not hurry to examine and leave.

She indicated that Diana could pass any day now.

My emotions are swirling within. After the nurse left, I cried as I sat alone with my love. I feel overwhelmed with grief. I know I need to keep it together to help my love pass with comfort and the joy that she's lived her wonderful life—our shared life. Her children and grandchildren have been the most evolved creations of her life—as well of course, her other fulfilling artistic expressions and lasting connections to friends, the loving care she gave to everything she touched with such depth, honesty, empathy, wisdom.

I looked at her and thought, *"I have to let you fly away. I need to prepare even as I continue to live in the moment with you—every moment will be a treasured memory."*

Until these last few weeks, I have not been thinking about what it will be like when Diana is gone, when I no longer can share with her, care for her—*when I can no longer look into your eyes and see you smile.*

I want to enjoy being with her in each moment I can, and then when it is time for her to go, I will assist her to pass in a graceful and comfortable way. Then after that I will deal with my grief.

I Have Never Experienced This Before...

...surrounded by the coming death of the love of my life—someone who is so much a part of me.

You, my love, are not just lying there in your hospice bed—you are existing in my soul, and when you pass, a part of me will pass—you will take a part of me with you, and how will I heal this loss of a part of my soul? We've shared so much during these past 41 years. Perhaps you could just take all of me with you—no, I know I need to remain in this realm, but maybe I can come visit you from time to time, and you will come to visit me...

...such wonderful thoughts comforting me with a spiritual possibility, an inter-dimensional hope.

Language of the Spirit Dimensions

Even if we only know one or a few languages, we also may not realize what we do know. I believe we exist in many dimensions and in various passages of time and timelessness. The experience of soon losing my love to another dimension in her afterlife has made me more conscious, more in tune with my belief in the multiple dimensions beyond our life here on earth. We are more varied and diverse than we know, even more so than our earth-based diversity allows us to be.

I want to explore the potentials of the beyond life, the afterlife, and even though I have never learned other languages well beyond the native born English, maybe in these other dimensions I can understand and communicate with the languages of the soul, heart, and spiritual imagination—through exquisite and meaningful imagery, receiving and sending out messages where no words need to be spoken.

Diana and I have always been able to communicate in this way—and even more so during this time when words for her have less and less meaning.

Separated and Connected

Diana, we are already separated in most ways in this world, yet we've remained connected in our souls. Your smile when you hear my voice, and when you see me. You may not always cognitively know who I am, but I can see and sense that somewhere in your psyche you know me and remain intertwined with me.

Even though we cannot communicate any longer with words, our communication transcends words and embraces what flows between our souls, conveyed through the loving gazes in our eyes.

The Last Days of Passing—Still Living Together in the Moment

I know Diana is in the last phase of her life here in this time-space reality. She is sleeping almost all the time, not eating or drinking much, and it is difficult for me to let go, even though I know this really is her passage. I want her to enter into the next dimension with comfort and openness, to transition well with joy and spiritual ease.

But I'm still feeling a growing sense of loss and disorientation. I realize my life has been so structured these past years of caregiving for her—so structured around her needs and the sharing of our love for each other in the most basic simple ways. I've never lived so fully in the moment as I have with Diana during these past five years—there has been no past or future in our communications—just what we have been experiencing in each moment.

This has been a gift because I have been able to experience the essence of Diana's wise and lovely being in each moment, and in ways that have brought us to even more transformative levels of emotional sharing.

Whistling to John Lennon's Song, "Jealous Guy"

Today when I was listening to "Jealous Guy," I remember even up until recently when Diana listened to this song, she knew when to start whistling to accompany John Lennon whistling in the song. She knew when to begin and when to end, and her whistling was so enjoyable to listen to. Just a few weeks ago, before Diana began to sleep more and seemed to be existing already in beyond life dimensions, I was sitting beside her as she lay in the hospice bed, and "Jealous Guy" came on. She had stopped singing along to the songs she loved like she used to. So I was surprised that when the whistling began in the song, she also started whistling and continued just like she had always done. I just sat listening with tears in my eyes. I wondered if this would be the last time she would whistle with John Lennon—at least in this earth realm.

Will We Meet Again?

What am I going to do without her? As much as this question brings deep emotions of loss and despair for me, I have been trying to prepare for this coming moment—a flood of memories come into my heart and mind. I have been involved with the life of an amazing and evolved woman.

Will we meet again? Will we be conscious of meeting in our past or future lives?

Whether that happens or not I cherish the experiences I've had with her and am still having and will have until the end of her passage. I want to let these feelings surround me, and then I want to blend these feelings with the joyful memories of present and past, while envisioning the future of our reconnecting as something that I'll always have to give me hope.

We Still Have Time for Sharing Sweet Moments

This early evening Diana has been awake—eating a little and responsive—with her eyes, her facial expression, her essence of being that just flows so sweetly from her. We're now listening to Pink Martini and having a special connection beyond words, and that is familiar and gratifying. She looked at me and smiled when I told her how much I loved her, how beautiful she is, how we're soul mates, and that she is my cosmic companion, the queen of my universe.

It is moments like this that lift my spirits and soothe my soul.

Going to a Movie by Myself (The Shape of Water)

Had a few hours this afternoon to spend by myself. I went to the gym for a treadmill work out until about 1:00 pm. Then drove downtown and parked near the Bijou Metro movie theater. I walked around looking for something to eat. My favorite Greek restaurant, Poppi's Anatolia, was closed. I wasn't in the mood for a hamburger. I finally bought a pizza slice and a side of salad.

But throughout my walk I had a bittersweet moment as I thought about how often Diana and I would take long walks together in different parts of Eugene, enjoying each other in silence as well as in lively conversations. And I thought that I would never be able to do this again with her. I tried to move on with my feelings, knowing that I have to be able to blend loss with sweet memories and appreciation of what life has given me with all these years of being able to walk together in life with my soul mate, in Eugene and throughout the cities of Europe.

As I walked back to where my car was parked, I decided to go see a movie. It was about 2:00pm, and I still had enough time before I needed to be home to take over for the caregiver who was with Diana. I decided to see The Shape of Water, which was showing at the Bijou Metro Movie Theater.

While sitting in the theater waiting for the movie to begin, I again had the realization that I would never again be going to a movie with Diana. I remembered the last time I was in this theater with her. We were watching a documentary about the early years when the Beatles were just becoming famous. The documentary showed their concerts, and as they sang Diana sang out loud with them. She seemed so engrossed and happy—it was delightful. The last movie I took her to was Wonder Woman. When the movie began, I could tell she was not even focusing on the movie screen. But one of the first scenes was of Wonder Woman as a child, running through the mythical village where she lived. Then a woman started calling her name, "Diana! Diana!" And as she did my Diana turned her attention to the movie screen for the first time, and raised her hand toward the screen as if she was saying, "Here I am. Here I am." She seemed peaceful after that, and she seemed comfortable during the rest of the movie, though not always looking at the screen. As we walked out, I realized that this would be the last movie I would take her to. She was having a difficult time walking, and I realized she had lost the ability to track anything that was going on in a movie.

The movie I watched this afternoon was just the right one for my mood. I thoroughly enjoyed this romantic, mythological film, the story of a woman connecting with a creature so different from her, yet transcending species, transcending dimensions to be able to breathe together within water—the lovely image of their bodies intertwined in the magic of the water has stayed with me.

I walked out of the theater into the sunshine, the first dry day of daylight savings, and I felt happy and satisfied. I will enjoy life while I am living and will always carry with me the love of my life. I know I still have some time to appreciate her presence. I will continue to embrace her in these moments, while still encouraging her to continue on her journey when she feels she's ready, and knowing I will be keeping her near my heart no matter where she travels to next. And perhaps somehow I will be able to connect with her again while I am still living and when I pass.

I Won't Let Go

I won't let go of my connection to you, the love of my life, beyond our lifetimes—I won't let go of the loving connection I have with your body-soul-spirit.

I won't let go of the interwoven threads of our inner essences, and I hope to continue to have the fabric of love that we have created to continue to warm our souls.

I Can Let Go

Of your physical presence, my love, because I have never felt I needed to cling to you, to possess you. I've felt ok about your choices even if they at times meant we were separated physically from each other for a while—like the times you went to Europe without me—working in the orphanages of Romania, or traveling around Europe with friends or family or just by yourself.

I know I can let go of you now, knowing that our connection will exist beyond this realm of being, even as we now will need to travel separately for... how long?

Diana, Can You Hear Me? Are You Still Breathing?

I just checked Diana—almost 9:00pm. She had her eyes closed while something—an ethereal quality of being—glowed through her skin tone, something of an essence of spiritual sensuality surrounding her body. She seemed so still. I bent and listened to see if I could hear her breathing. She was breathing—softly. I put my hand on her chest and felt her heartbeat, and felt a joy of relief

Earlier in the evening before she normally goes to sleep for the night, I wanted to gently see if I could wake her. I said, *"Diana, can you hear me?"* Nothing, no response.

I gently stroked the top of her head, feeling her lovely thick, slightly greying black hair. *"Diana, I love you. Can you hear me?"* Nothing.

I very softly stroked her cheek. *"Diana, I love you. Can you hear me?"*

"Yes!" She opened her eyes and looked at me, first without an expression—she went in and out of closing and opening her eyes.

"Hi Diana. Do you know how much I love you?"

She turned her head slowly and we looked into each other's eyes. We held each other's gaze for a few moments. Then she smiled! After a few seconds she turned her head away and closed her eyes again.

These are such precious moments! But I will let her drift away back into sleep or beyond. I decided I won't be asking her if she can hear me any longer when she is sleeping. I won't try to wake her any longer. She needs to have encouragement and peace as she moves into her next journey.

Though I will enjoy remembering these precious moments of her connecting with me with her lovely gaze and her smile!

Diana Talks a Little, Expresses Concerns

Diana has been awake on and off today, and a few minutes ago her expression seemed to convey worry. She has not been speaking these past few days, but at one point today she spoke. She asked about her mother who had passed away 18 years ago. She asked if the kids were ok and expressed concern about not being able to be with them. She also said, "I don't seem to be able to do anymore what needs to be done."

I tried to communicate that everyone was ok, and that she could relax now. I told her she has done so much for others all through her life, and that it's time for to relax a bit. I told her she would be able to be active and continue doing things she loved soon.

I want her to pass in peace. I was trying to comfort her as well as me. I want her to know I'll remain with her in my thoughts and feelings, and in my heart, soul, and spirit.

I Will Need Time to Adjust

Diana is sleeping. I've had so much wonderful support for my caregiving from family, friends, and the special caregivers that I have found to help. But I know soon, I will be alone in this physical reality.

I will need time to adjust. Despite all of the support and expressions of love and support for Diana and myself—I know I will need some time by myself, knowing that I will never be or feel isolated.

I am surrounded by the love of my family and the caring thoughts of my friends. I also know that Diana's presence will always be surrounding me—in sweet memories, and in connections I hope to have from her wherever she is in her journeys through other dimensions of the afterlife.

Maybe I can follow her, be with her again in some ways even while I am living in my time on earth. I'm determined to try when I am ready—when I have transformed the deep grief I am and will be feeling.

Diana Drifting Away—seeming Distant—yet at Peace

As I was telling Diana goodnight, she seemed different—distant—I told her how much I love her and talked softly and gently to her about how grateful I am that she has chosen to share her life with me. I also told her I wanted to remain a part of her life, to embrace this next phase of her existence beyond this life.

Throughout our time together, we've blended our destinies, while also encouraging each other to continue to become all of whom we were individually meant to be in this lifetime. Sometimes I wonder how I can continue being who I am meant to be without her, but then I immediately know I will continue to be and develop who I am meant to be because of her.

Diana is dying, will soon be passing into other dimensions, where I will join her in ways I can, to continue going together on loving, shared journeys and adventures, sharing moments somehow as she exists in the afterlife.

Diana, my love, you seem at such peace now, as you seem to be existing more and more in beyond life dimensions, even as you continue coming back here for precious brief connections with me and your loved ones in this reality. I am cherishing each moment you are remaining with me. You are and will always be my cosmic love through all dimensions.

Her Next Journey

I love the concept of her taking off, flying away into other wonderful destinations beyond the here and now—reuniting with old friends and family who have also journeyed away from this lifetime on earth, but also perhaps interacting with other spirit guides like her—who some refer to as gods or goddesses. I believe her own spiritual development will be enough to give her light to see where she is at all times, beyond time.

As these feelings flow through my psyche and heart, I want to let her know that she will be taking a love connection with her as she begins her new journeys. I hope that any beyond life connections we are able to make will add a little more warmth and joy to her journey.

What Will I Do in the Days after She Passes?

I will take off from my work. I will be preparing for Diana's Celebration of Life. Family and close friends will be helping me prepare for celebrating Diana's life on earth and assisting her in continuing her spiritual journey where I hope to one day share experiences with her again. I've been so fortunate to be living in the moment with her.

My life will be changing.

Magical Day

The hospice social worker came today and sat by Diana and read a lovely poem with a gentle and soothing voice. Later the hospice harp player came by and sang and played songs for Diana, who seemed to flow in and out of awareness, but seemed at peace within the ambience of the music.

Spring Equinox—Endings and Beginnings

It will be occurring at 9:15am PDST today—The Sun will be transiting from Pisces into Aires—the end of one annual cycle of time in this reality, and the beginning of a new cycle of opportunities for unfolding ourselves and our potentials.

The energy we can draw upon relates to spontaneity, to bursts of new options, hopes, directions—a freshness of spring colors and scents within our gardens and within our psyches.

I know that Diana's life on this earth is ending. She remains in this reality, but I feel that most of her has already transcended into a new phase of being. I love her so much, but I want to help her in any way I can to transition well into dimensions beyond the cycles of seasons and time.

My Life Without You

I know my life is changing, also. I am transitioning into my own new cycle of being, and I know I will have to begin this new phase without you physically present in this reality that we have both been sharing.

I want to continue the lifestyle we have both embraced—to savor the ways we lived our lives together each day—the types of food and meals we ate, the music we listened to, the incense and candles we lit to enhance the scents and light within our living spaces, the walks we went on throughout the neighborhood and city, the gardening and chores we did together, and the loving interactions we had with our children and grandchildren and close friends. I intend on continuing this lifestyle, only you will not be physically present in a way that I can hold you in my arms, hold your hand as we walk together, dance with you, and make love.

I want to slowly look through all your personal belongings to identify what I want to keep around me—your art, your journals and sketch books, special scarves and other small clothing items you chose to reflect your essence and moods, the special cookbooks, and other books that have meant so much to you.

As I live my daily life continuing to experience all the things we loved doing together, I will be experiencing you as part of me in my daily life.

The Caregiving I Will No Longer Need to Do

I'm happy that Diana continues to be present in this reality, still with me—she is still breathing, but mostly she stays asleep.

This morning I peeled some mandarin oranges and took the skin off of the apple I was going to cut up. I started peeling the skin off of the apple because Diana had become confused about having to chew food that did not dissolve easily, and she would just take the food she found difficult to chew out of her mouth and set it on the table.

For a moment, I felt a deep sadness, as I reflected on how many mornings I have made breakfast for her over these last few years. I felt the emotions of loss flow through me, but then I thought, *I'm doing this for you now and I will continue to do this for you and me, my love, after you go on your way. I will continue to do this and experience our love by doing these simple daily activities.*

A little while later, I felt the same emotion of loss while I was folding clothes that I had just washed and dried, some of hers, some of mine. I folded one of the cotton ponchos that Tracy had bought for her last year because it was getting difficult for me to remove and put on her shirts, jackets, and coats any longer. It was just too awkward to assist her to put her arms through the sleeves, and it was so much easier to just slide the poncho over her head. As I folded her clothes, I realized I would never need to wash, dry, and fold these clothes any longer now that she was always wearing her hospital gown.

This awareness that my caregiving activities would soon not be needed any longer triggered a flow of tears at my coming loss of Diana.

Suspended in Time

I feel uneasy tonight. Why do I feel so uneasy?

I've been preparing for your passing, and yet I know as it's coming closer. I feel inside me a resistance, the fear of experiencing the loss of your physical presence in my life. I feel like moments of time have come to a standstill, as I wait for you to make your choice to go, and I do want you to go on your journey unhindered and with joy.

I am Overwhelmed by the Coming Loss of Diana in My Life

The loss of being able to gaze into your lovely eyes.
The loss of listening to our special music together.
The loss of making love with you.
The loss of hearing you laugh, sing, and dance.
The loss of being in conversation with you about the children and grandchildren's lives, about the joys and challenges of our daily life together, of our house maintenance, of Ayurveda foods and healing, of metaphysics, of astrology, of the travels we've been on, of new adventures we want to take.

I grieve the loss of your touch, your wisdom, your creativity.

I grieve the loss of how you make life so magical in so many ways.

I grieve the loss of my physical, sensual, mental, emotional, soul, and spiritual connection with you.

I know that the sweet memories of our life together in all of these ways will bring comfort to me, and a fulfilling appreciation of the gift of being able to create so many wonderful memories with you.

But I am overwhelmed by the sense of loss I know is coming any moment now.

Diana Transcended

Diana passed earlier today.

I will be spending time alone as I grieve the losses I will be experiencing, and to eventually prepare to journey into my inner world to connect with the soul of the love of my life in a peaceful and magical way. I hope one day soon I will be able and ready to journey into the afterlife to fulfill my promise.

But now my time of grieving and adjustment begins.

Part IV

The Weeks After She Passed— Transforming My Grieving Celebrating Diana's Essence and Our Time Together

When the darkness of grief has lifted from my soul, the light of our enduring love will guide me to find you again, my love.

I know in my heart, I will be able to move beyond my grief of losing the physical presence of your being while I remain alive—and then I will be able to develop the spiritual capacities to journey into the afterlife to be with you again.

Diana Transitioned from This Earth Realm Last Night, and Today Is My 73rd Birthday

Diana is no longer physically here on earth, but I woke up this morning feeling her soul and love within my heart. I will be comforted by the memories of our dynamic life we shared together. My time of sharing life with her physical presence has ended right before my birth day.

As an astrologer I am aware that birthdays are a time for reflection of an individual's inner potentials and how one is actualizing these potentials. Astrologers cast special charts called a Solar Return Chart at the moment when the Sun returns to the exact degree and minute of the sign it was at the time of birth. While the Sun will be in its placement at birth, everything else in the chart will be different and will reflect the year's moment of rebirth, and tell a story of the coming year for the individual—opportunities, challenges, and areas of focus that might be beneficial.

I have not cast my Solar Return for this year yet, but today I will be reflecting about the endings and beginnings I am experiencing—physical death and the rebirth of consciousness in beyond life dimensions. I want to spend the day surrounded by memories of Diana, I want to focus on wishing her well on her own new journey, and I want to try to embrace my own new beginnings on my birthday as I know she would want me to.

Removing Diana's Body and the Hospice Bed–an Empty Space

A couple of men from the funeral home came over last night to take Diana's body to be cremated. Just a few minutes ago the medical equipment company came and picked up the hospice bed.

I'm sitting in the soft white cloth swivel chair in the empty space between the two built-in benches that were on both sides of the hospice bed on which Diana had been lying during these past weeks. Being in this empty space makes everything so real, and I feel deeply shaken uncomfortably out of a numbing trance. I realize I had been acting on auto-pilot in my consciousness since she passed not even twenty-four hours ago—contacting the family, contacting the funeral home, contacting the medical equipment company, going to sleep last night in a daze, waking up this morning in a state of numbness. I've been in a trance, perhaps a protective trance—but now the reality of what's happened has been brought into an intense focus as I'm sitting here alone in this empty space. A feeling of profound emptiness has come over me—she's gone, the bed is gone—it seems like everything is gone… and I can only sit here and cry, feeling the tears for the first time since she passed.

I had just put on the CD player a disc I had made of some of our favorite songs, and as I sat with my feelings of loss overwhelming me now in this now empty space, I heard the soft, intense beginning of Pink Floyd's "Shine On You

Crazy Diamond" start playing—almost as though Diana was playing this song for me, and I began to instantly feel comforted.

I still sat with tears in my eyes, but I began to feel a release, as I listened to the instrumental beginning slowly unfold and surround me. My feelings of emptiness were being transformed as I listened. I felt the power of the instruments synthesizing and building with intensity and reminding me that this space in which we had lived together was not really empty, and my life would never be empty. I was being reminded that I had not lost Diana, just her physical presence, and she remains with me now, shining in my consciousness and my soul.

I stood up and lit one of the candles that sat on the cabinet in the front part of the room, then looked back at the empty living space between the two built-in benches. I would soon be replacing this empty space with the long, light, solid maple table Diana had designed and asked a local woodworker to build when we first started living together. This table represents so many wonderful memories that have filled our lives with gatherings of family and friends and mostly just the two of us over the years. I smiled, imagining this empty space again being filled with the long light wood table for future gatherings and a place to share love and stories—as it has been and will continue to be.

It's Been Both a Difficult and Somehow Uplifting Day

I've had meandering feelings and thoughts throughout this day, my birthday. It's evening, and I will try to go to sleep with these varieties of emotions—some causing me to cry with such a sadness of loss, and then changing into the joy of remembrances and appreciations of the opportunity to share 41 years with such a soul mate— I've been so fortunate. Am I so selfish that I can't let go, that I want more?

But I just miss her so much. I know I will have so many of these mood swings for a while, and I want to stay with all of the feelings as they flow through me. I know I will be able to embrace my future in time. I know I have the strength. I hope so. This is maybe the most difficult thing I've had to face in my life… building my life anew without the love of my life.

My Cosmic Companion

What do I mean when I call you my cosmic companion, Diana, my love? I mean that you have been my life partner and lover who have traveled with me across the limits of space and time in this world. Together we have allowed each other to transcend the separateness of our individual beings to become one in so many sweet, passionate, and challenging moments of intimacy. And now as you've moved on into your next journey into other dimensions, I hope I will be able to join you again, my cosmic companion, to continue our intimate adventures and love.

I felt these passionate, spiritual—cosmic—qualities in you when I first met you—and sharing life with you has given me the opportunity to develop some of these qualities within myself. By the time I met you I was beginning to be satisfied that I was developing a comprehensive and holistic understanding of a model of life in our time frame on earth that was meaningful to me. You showed me something more—you existed so well in this earth realm, but you showed me the magic and beauty that comes from somewhere else. From a dimension that transcends time and space, transcends biases, polarities, and conflicts of imbalanced perceptions. You did this with a soul that communicated with such compassion and empathy and soft strength.

From the moment I first met you, there was something you seemed to nurture in my heart, and I know you have connected with others in this way. There has always been something in how you engage with others that transcends the mind, transcends memory—that just flows from your heart, from the loving and compassionate spirit of your being.

You've been my cosmic companion all these years, and I think we have gifted each other's insights within the exquisite union of love. I know that I will eventually find you in whatever beyond life reality you exist in. You are my cosmic companion. And I hope you also keep trying to find me!

Planning for the Celebration of Life Ceremony

Diana had such a good life and transitioned in such a good way, a peaceful way. I like the words, "transitioned" and "transcended"—because I believe in multiple and simultaneous beyond life realities or dimensions in the spirit world that people transition into when they leave this earth in the process we call death. But it is not really death, if that means ceasing to exist—though I realize it is meant to mean ceasing to exist in the individual's current earth body. I believe the consciousness of a being continues to exist after physically leaving this earth realm.

Tracy, my oldest daughter, and I will be identifying a space to have this celebration of life. I'm not particularly interested in having it in a church. One place would be the Tsunami Bookstore, which has a stage and quite a capacity for seating. Another place I've thought about is Theo's Coffee House (what used to be Cozmic Pizza). It has a stage, and Diana and I attended events there often, especially when they had concerts celebrating the birthdays of George Harrison and John Lennon.

Tracy and I decided we'd also go to the University of Oregon to see if we could identify a suitable space there. Diana is an old soul—she touched and enhanced all our souls. I want the space chosen to celebrate her life to be reflective of her essence of being.

Forgetting I've Been Released from My Caregiving

For a moment tonight as I lay down to go to sleep, I wondered when I would need to get up to give Diana her medication. Then I realized that my caregiving had ended. I was released from needing to care for the love of my life. I felt such sadness. I didn't want to be released from providing caregiving to her—but I embraced the thought that I am choosing to never be released from caring for her spirit, even if I no longer need to care for her body.

Replacing the Hospice Bed with Our Long Light Wooden Table

Today Marc, my son-in-law, helped me bring the long light wood, western maple table back into the front room, and helped me set it up in the empty space between the two built-in benches. I placed a variety of framed photos of Diana at one end of the 8 ft. table. I would be sitting at the other end as I eat my meals now that Diana is not sitting in that space eating her meals. I placed, near the photographs, the heart candles I had given Diana years ago on Valentine's Day (our anniversary of when we started living together). We only lit one of the heart-shaped candles briefly, and we decided to never light them again so they could be kept as symbols of our love.

As I gazed at that end of the table, I realized I did not want to look closely at the framed photographs of Diana. I was not ready to see her again so alive and in a way that would remind so deeply that I could never again experience sharing with her in these ways–at least, not in this physical earth realm.

Death Should Not Be about Just What Has Been Lost

We often resist recognizing other dimensions beyond death because of what patriarchal, controlling religions want us to fear.

Beyond what we think of what might exist in the afterlife, I believe there is nothing to fear in beyond life dimensions. Too often the death of loved ones leaves behind guilt and ongoing grief that should be transformed into joy for those who have transitioned and who are now living a transcended life. Too often what we have been told about death leaves behind feelings of loss and inner pain. This is certainly what I am feeling now, but even as I grieve my loss, I know Diana is flowing well within beyond life dimensions, and I know I have not really lost her.

Many people in our culture do not seem to appreciate that those who move on into the exquisite afterlife are living in transcendent dimensions of infinite spiritual possibilities and joy. In contemplating on the death of my love partner, I know I want to focus on hope for cosmic healing and contentment for our loved ones who have passed. I want to be reflecting on these thoughts and feelings now—not just the grief that Diana's death has left behind for me—not just my selfish feelings of sorrow.

What Do I Know and Don't Know about Loss and Love?

I have to admit, I haven't explored all these concepts of life. I don't know everything—well maybe most everything, because I sit almost every night watching a blend of Fox News, MSBN, and CNN—just joking. I'm actually watching the latest marvel movie in between commercials of whatever sports game is on—again just kidding, sort of. The main shows I watch are reruns of Star Trek The Next Generation and Star Trek Voyager. I think these two series should win a Nobel Prize for the most uplifting expressions of the evolved possibilities for our human societies—all the Nobel Prizes combined. The stories of these shows always reflect humans and sometimes other alien races rising above the base instincts of life forms to find compassionate, intelligent solutions to conflicts and insecurities and biases of galactic and beyond galactic proportions. What century did earth achieve that? Well, I won't be alive in this earth realm to experience this, yet I do see the beginning. I am an internal optimist. But what do I know?

All I really know in actual terms (whatever that means), I am experiencing the streams of the love of cosmic proportions. I am experiencing the streams of the loss of my best friend, my lover, my cosmic companion, my soul mate—yet the sense of loss can be understood only as a spiritual gift of love that I can know by my memories, and maybe also by future intentions full of desires to reconnect. I know what I can't explain rationally, but the most exquisite knowledge exists in what we know beyond rationally, and if we are lucky we would be able to know consciously and with a loving sensuality, if not always in each moment, but at least in our memories. But I do remember. That's what I am happy to know, even if I don't know everything.

You are Dancing in My Soul

I'm sitting in my green chair listening to Pink Martini singing Omide Zendegani, and I feel you, Diana—I feel you are dancing with me in my soul, I feel you are freeing my consciousness from the limits of this earth realm to dance with you in ways I have never danced before. I can visualize you in the rhythms of this music, in the imagination of my memories of our love. I see you, feel you dancing with me, and you give me so much joy tonight, allowing me to rise above my feelings of loss. I feel you are dancing within my soul.

Hidden Treasures and Opportunities– Finding an Amazing Room for Diana's Celebration of Life

Today Tracy and I went looking at spaces for Diana's celebration of life. We first went to the Tsunami Bookstore, and we had a good feeling about its natural atmosphere. We had attended a number of poetry readings, musical events, and metaphysical presentations, including astrologer Johanna Mitchell's fundraiser each January where she gave a colorful forecast for the coming year.

We decided to visit more places before making our final decision. We both agreed we wanted to go to the University of Oregon and see if they had a room that would have an ambience we were looking for.

At the University of Oregon, we met with the Director of Student Services at the Erb Memorial Union. The Erb Memorial Union had been remodeled a few years earlier, and I had attended a few concerts and presentations in some of their large rooms. We were shown various rooms that had light wood floors and large modern windows which brought in bright, warm light from the outside, but neither Tracy nor I connected with the ambience of these rooms. We went back to the director's office so that he could give us the details of the costs and availability in case we decided to choose one of these rooms. However, he could tell we were not that excited about any of the rooms we had seen.

At one point, he looked at us and said, "I'd like to show you another room. It's actually one of my favorite rooms at the University of Oregon. It's the Gerlinger Lounge in the Gerlinger Hall building across the street. I was thinking you wanted to have a room in this Erb Memorial Building, but I think this other room would be what you are looking for."

He led us across the street and into the front entrance of Gerlinger Hall, built in 1919. He led us across the large foyer with marble floors and high ceilings to a stairway which after the first few steps split into two stairways curving back to the entrance of a room on the second floor above the foyer.

As we walked into this large rectangular room, I knew instantly this was where Diana would have wanted to have her celebration of life ceremony. On both ends of the room were fireplaces with dark wood mantles. To either side of the fireplace were large wood-framed windows. There were couches and easy chairs in front of both fireplaces, and further in toward the center of the room, long antique tables enclosed the two seating areas and created a center space where over a hundred folding chairs could be set up. This center area had a large Persian rug covering the floor. This beautiful rug, with soft red patterns of flowers and geometric shapes woven into the magenta colored background, was the kind of rug Diana had purchased over the years for various areas of our house. The ceiling lights were incandescent, in simple but classical ornate fixtures reflective of past times when buildings were designed with more of a European feel. On all the windows were long dark thick cloth curtains that could be pulled aside to let light in. In front of the center area was a podium, and the student services director said that if we wanted to rent this room, he would provide a media assistant who would set up a screen and co-ordinate any visual and sound systems we would want.

Tracy felt the same way I did about this room. It was exactly what we were looking for. The south side of this room looked out over the Pioneer Cemetery that had existed since 1872. A block further south from the cemetery was where Diana and I lived from 1979 to 1999. We had moved into our Tiara Street house the fall before, but several of the kids still stayed at the house helping to care for my mother until she died on Mother's Day, 1999.

The strange thing about Gerlinger Lounge is that even though I completed two degrees at the University of Oregon (BA in English Literature from 1963-1967 and MA in Counseling Psychology from 1978 to 1980), and Diana had taken art classes at the university from the time she moved to Eugene in 1975 until completing her BA in Fine Arts in 1980, and despite the fact that we had lived so close and spent so much time at events and just walking around the campus over the years, neither one of us had been in this room or even knew it existed.

This seemed to reaffirm my belief that hidden treasures and meaningful opportunities exist all around us, waiting for us to make efforts to look deeper, to explore further than what we can see on the surface and spaces surrounding us.

As I came home, feeling so happy, I realized that now I wanted to focus on the ceremony itself—the music, a slide show of some of Diana's art, and the gathering of photos and canvasses and drawings of her actual art pieces.

I Dreamed that I Would be Dying During the Coming Day

During the middle of last night, I had a dream that someone came to tell me I would be passing at 4:30am. I remember feeling that I did not want to die yet, but I also felt peaceful about it, and hopeful that I would be with Diana.

I woke up from my dream to see what time it was–1:00am. I remembered my dream. I don't usually remember the specifics of my dreams, even if I sometimes wake with the vague awareness of having dreamed. But this dream was vivid in my half-awake, half-dream state. As I thought about the dream, I became unsure of whether I was told I'd be passing at 4:30am or 4:30pm. I shook my head, thinking how could I be confused about that?

So I thought if it was 4:30am, I would only have a few hours left to live. And then I thought to myself, "Well, let's see." I went back to sleep. Sometime later in the night, I remember waking again briefly, wondering if this was my time to pass, and if this is the time, it's ok.

When I woke up again it was a little after 7:00am. I felt a relief at seeing the light of the early morning shining though the edges of the shades on the windows near my bed. Yet I lay in my bed in a contemplative mood, reflecting on why did something in my psyche or someone in another realm come to tell me I would be passing from this life. Could it have been Diana—I just could not bring the image into my mind of the entity or person who told me I would be dying. Maybe it was Diana, and she was just communicating with me that she wanted to see me and hoped that I could find her soon. Then I knew that Diana would really want me to continue living my life in a full way.

As I lay half awake, I had this feeling that I was caught between realities, with part of my consciousness not wanting to leave this life yet, and another part of my consciousness wanting so much to enter the beyond life realms that Diana was now existing in.

A little bit later as I was writing this dream down in my journal and sipping my morning coffee, I remembered that when I woke earlier, I had been unclear whether I had been told I would be passing at 4:30am or 4:30pm. I was surprised that I began feeling a sense of apprehension. This was not over. Then I smiled to myself, thinking this was my cosmic companion playing with me. My rational earth mind knew it was a dream and I would not be dying. Yet something in my psyche remained a little unsure. All I could do was go about my day and see what would be happening.

At 4:30pm, I was actually having a beer by myself at the Bier Stein, sitting by the fireplace in the back area where Diana and I would sit together from time to time. She liked the Bier Stein because it reminded her of the guest houses of Bavaria, with its large areas and horseshoe bar in the middle. There were even banners and posters on the walls with symbols of Bavaria. Diana didn't drink that much beer, but there was always a German Heifeweizen on tap, and she would drink a small glass, especially if we were sharing an appetizer of bratwurst, sauerkraut, and bretzel.

I was lost in this reverie of Diana and sharing these moments together, when I suddenly wondered what time it was. I looked up at the clock on the wall and saw that it was a little past 4:30pm. I laughed to myself, thinking I survived. Was this just a cosmic joke? Again, I had the thought of Diana playfully communicating with me.

But then I became more thoughtful and began to appreciate how special this dream was. I don't remember my dreams every often, and yet this dream was so real, so powerful, and made me feel at times that I actually might die, first at 4:30am and then, when I didn't die at that time, at 4:30pm. All through these hours, I had to focus on and be torn about not wanting to leave this earth life, and yet desiring to move on and connect again with the love of my life.

I realized that being with Diana in my thoughts and memories during these last days and weeks had increased my intention to make use of each moment of time that I still exist in this realm. But also, this dream had increased my intention to develop my capacity to journey into beyond life realms, to reconnect with Diana and to visit her from time to time in both my dream and waking states.

Preparing for the Celebration of Life

The celebration of life ceremony for Diana is tomorrow. I have been going non-stop this past week, and I know I will need to continue planning and organizing right up to the ceremony. I've been trying to step away for a few moments at times to center my emotions on memories of Diana and her soul presence. I want so much for this gathering to reflect her lovely and spiritual essence.

I didn't realize what an undertaking this would be to plan a celebration of life ceremony for perhaps over a hundred family and friends. I am so fortunate that I've had sustained and caring help, though. Our close friend Karen who lives near Seattle came into town a week before the celebration to help. She and our youngest daughter Madeline have been going through our many boxes of photographs that have accumulated over the 76 years of Diana's life and the 41 years Diana and I have been together. These photographs reflect memories of our children and grandchildren, our relationship, our friends from around the world and here in the Tiara Street Community. Karen and Madeline created ten poster boards with titles such as *Diana's Early Family, Diana and Mark (2), Diana and her Children (2), Diana and her Grandchildren (2), Diana and Friends (3).* Then they pasted photographs related to the titles. It was quite time-consuming, and Karen and Madeline did this so well. My older brother John and my younger brother Mike and his wife Jill had also come into town and were helping with last minute things to do.

I created two playlists of our special music for the ceremony. The playlist I wanted played as people entered the room before the ceremony would begin consisted of serene and romantic world music that reflected Diana's spiritual and romantic essence—music by such artists as Luciano Pavarotti, Andrea Bocelli, I Muvrini, and Priyo. Then I created a playlist I planned to play after the ceremony finished as people would be visiting and walking around looking at the photographs and Diana's art. This playlist consisted of songs such as George Harrison's *My Sweet Lord,* Neil Young's *Heart of Gold,* and Eric Clapton's *Layla.* I felt these songs, while also romantic, were also more upbeat.

I also planned on playing a slide show of Diana's art on a large screen before and after the ceremony.

But I ran into technical problems. My desktop where all my music and photographs are stored is a PC, but I needed to transfer the playlists and slide show onto my Mac Air laptop so that it could be synched with media equipment in the U of O Gerlinger Lounge. I didn't know how to make the transfer, but fortunately my friend and computer technician, Doug Hoss, came over this evening at the last minute and made the transfer. He also agreed to be available at the ceremony to coordinate with the U of O media assistant and make sure the media activities would flow smoothly. I felt appreciative and relieved that this aspect of the celebration seemed to be handled.

As these practical aspects of the ceremony were being

taken care of, I was also focused on my role. I planned on sharing my thoughts and feelings at the beginning, and then I would ask our oldest granddaughter Whitney if she would take around the wireless microphone to those who wanted to share their own thoughts and feelings about Diana. I'm feeling excited with the anticipation of celebrating with others the wonderful and unique soul that Diana embodied and shared with all those with whom she interacted.

The Celebration of Life Ceremony

I had scheduled the Gerlinger Lounge for the ceremony from 1:00 to 3:00pm. About an hour before the ceremony our family and close friends began setting up the room. Diana's actual paintings and drawings and the 10 poster boards of photographs were placed in the areas around the room, on either side of the fireplaces and on other tables. An area for cookies, tea, and coffee was set up. Doug was working with the U of O media assistant to make sure the music and slide show were ready to be played. Someone at the U of O had placed more than a hundred chairs in the center of the room on the large, beautiful Persian rug. In front of the chairs was the screen for the slide show and also the podium.

When Whitney arrived, she agreed to take the wireless microphone around to people who wanted to share. But she asked me if she could give her own speech after I made my opening remarks, and I told her I'd love for her to do that. She said she was going to sit by herself before the ceremony began and write her speech. I felt excited to hear what she was going to say.

As people were coming into the room, I stood by the podium taking some deep breaths to calm myself. I had started the first playlist and the slideshow of Diana's artwork. I looked around and felt Diana's actual paintings, drawings, and the photographs of her life enhanced the room's magical ambience. I also began to feel a sense of peace and loving goodwill with the growing presence of the family and the close and causal friends who were coming into the room to celebrate Diana's life. All the chairs were occupied and there were other people standing around the room.

When I was ready to begin the ceremony, I turned off the music and the slide show. I welcomed everyone who had come. I described the magical and peaceful way Diana passed. I shared some special memories of our relationship. I described how Diana and I had met at the Saturday Market in the spring of 1976, when we both had separate booths across from each other—her selling batik clothes she had sewn, and me providing astrological readings. I described how fortunate I have always felt to have been invited into her life and share in the raising of her five wonderful children. I mentioned briefly about the joy of traveling together with her and sharing our creative projects.

I expressed how grateful I was for the assistance I had received from the family, neighbors, friends, caregivers, and hospice workers. At the end of my talk, I shared a well-known poem, A Native American Prayer. A copy of the poem had been given to me by Putzi before she left on a pre-arranged trip to Arizona. This poem had been sent to Putzi to give to me by a woman who had only met Diana once, but who felt she had a psychic connection to her:

Native American Prayer

I give you this one thought to keep
I am with you still, I do not sleep

I am a thousand winds that blow
I am the diamond glints on snow

I am the sunlight on ripened grain
I am the gentle autumn rain

When you awaken in the morning's hush
I am the swift, uplifting rush,
of quiet birds in circled flight

I am the soft stars that shine at night

Do not think of me as gone
I am with you still, in each new dawn.

I then introduced Whitney and explained she would be taking a microphone around for those who wanted to share, but that first she wanted to say a few words about her Oma. She came to the podium and gave the following speech that she had just written:

Oatmeal

My Oma. A little woman with a large, beautiful impression. The first memories that flood into my memory are the mornings I spent waking up snuggled deeply under a heavy, soft linen, goose feathered down comforter. One that had probably had been in our family for decades. Oma was practical about her possessions. Everything held a purpose, was of quality and would last years by the way she took care of it. So there I was, fighting the sunlight pressing against the back of my eye lids, But I couldn't hold out for long against the sweet, intoxicating smell of Oma's oatmeal. Oma's breakfast presentation was a perfect depiction of how she operated her life. Everything she did had intention, beauty and love at the core. I would wobble my way onto the wooden benches that held the small bottoms of all my cousins and me. Elbows knocking, long johns on and sleep stuck in the corner of our eyes. The table would be set with beautiful embroidered napkins, GiGi junes silverwear and plates, organic jams, ghee butter, pumpkin & nut topping, the classic glass jar of maple syrup with crystal resedue spilling over the sides. I'd often slide my greedy little finge across for a quick taste of the sweet goodness.

Opas toast was in rotation as he was
quickly buttering while sipping his bitter
black coffee, the way I take mine now, black
and the stronger the better. The stacks
of toast began to pile, and oma at the
oven, wooden spoon in hand, stirring as she
sprinkled fairy dust of cinnamon and nutmeg
blessing the oatmeal
A simple breakfast became the highlight of
the day, as it should be.
Oma knowing the importance of family, love
and sharing the peaceful vibrations of a
morning together
Oatmeal, a food that now lines the grocery store
isles with tag lines shouting
        "quick oats, only takes a minute"
        "grab and go"
        "on the run, oatmeal the perfect meal"
I want to make a vow here that I'll try to
never purchase one of these cop out meals.
See for me Oatmeal is now not just a food
item, but a metaphor for endless mornings
of love, created by her with a message she
often tried to teach me in her actions and words
        "Take your time Whitney, this is where
            the beauty lies"
                — My oma

As I listened to Whitney's speech about her Oma making oatmeal and breakfast on many occasions, I remembered some photographs I took of them sitting around
our long table. Madeline was helping out while Diana

was serving the breakfast. These photographs captured the many joyful moments we had with our grandchildren as they were growing up.

Remy, Lexi, Whitney, Sofia, Jasmine, Wyatt

Now sitting alone at home, I am savoring all the loving expressions that were shared during the ceremony, and how I believe the totality of the environment of room, the music, the displays, the teamwork of all us working together—allowed for the type of celebration of life that reflected all the wonderful unique qualities of Diana as an earth mother, as an Oma, as an artist, as a healer, as world traveler, as gardener, and as the love of my life.

What Will I Do Now, Where Will I Go Next?

It's been a few days since the celebration. The family and friends who came to share with me and attend the celebration of life have left Eugene to return to their homes, and the family and friends who live in Eugene have returned to their own life routines. Sitting alone in our living space where Diana passed—feeling a mixture of sadness and sereneness—I feel comforted being in this living space where I've experienced fulfilling and happy moments with Diana, my love.

I am wondering what will I do now, where I go next in my life? I don't need to know now, of course. I don't need an answer. I will discover the next phase of my life, evolve into the next phase. I want to allow myself to unfold in time, with Diana as my spirit guide, who has been my cosmic companion through our life together. I need to rely on the wisdom and love she gave as we helped each other develop within ourselves.

I will go where my heart guides me-where I've been

preparing to go throughout my life—with Diana's support, help, and guidance.

But for now, I am just content to sit alone, alone in the space she created, feeling embraced by all of the comforting living art with which she imbued our living space, as she did every space on earth she lived within. I smile as the beneficiary of her lovely creativity in life.

The Photographs of Diana at the Other End of the Long Table

When I get up each morning and sit at the one end of the long table to eat my breakfast, I still avoid looking at the framed photographs I've placed at the other end of the table 8 feet away. They are conveniently sitting far enough away that I don't have to look at them closely.

I continue to avoid looking at these wonderful photographs because it is still too painful for me to see her image, her presence displayed so fully, to see her smiles, her happiness, being near me, touching me sometimes, holding hands, standing so near each other, embracing each other.

Even though I cannot now bring myself to closely look at the photographic reminders of the love of my life as she lived in this world as my partner and lover, I do not want to put these photographs away at this time. I want to know all these images of her are sitting over there waiting for me to find the peace within me to enjoy the memories and feelings these photographs will evoke in me. I know that time will come when my resistances and profound sense of loss will be transformed. When I am able to enjoy looking at the real-life images of her and feel the joy, I know I will be ready to focus not just on my grieving, my self-oriented feelings of loss. I will be able to begin living fully during my own remaining time on earth. I know I will then be ready to begin the process of developing my abilities to enter into beyond life realms to find her, to reconnect with her more directly, and to fulfill the promise I made to her.

The Music We Listened to so Much Together

During the day and evenings before Diana would go to sleep, we would listen to music on the CD player or on Alexa. We listened often to Pink Martini, songs from George Harrison's *All Things Must Pass* album, songs from John Lennon, Pavarotti, Bocelli, Italian singers such as Zucchero, and Francesco De Gregori. We listened to the Corsica band I Muvrini and the Brazilian singer Marissa Monte. We listened to Eric Clapton's "Layla," Bob Dylan songs such as "Lay Lady Lay," and "I'll Be Your Baby Tonight."

I have not felt inclined to listen to most of the music Diana and I listened to so often. Again, I figured this resistance would be temporary, but I knew, just like seeing her in photographs, listening to the music we listened to every day together was too emotionally painful for me now.

Yet there were two exceptions. Every morning when I woke, I asked Alexa to play music by Andrea Bocelli, which I listened to as I drank my morning coffee, ate my breakfast, and got dressed. Then each night before I went to bed, I asked Alexa to play music by Pink Martini. For these past few years, I had been asking Alexa to play this music each morning and each evening while Diana was lying in bed before she went to sleep. As I lay with her before she drifted off to sleep, she would be listening to Pink Martini's different world music, moving her fingers and sometimes her feet to the rhythms of the music.

Continuing these morning and night rituals of music listening has been comforting to me, and I may continue beginning and ending these days with these same musical rituals indefinitely.

I am open to find new music that would not be so closely linked to the music we loved listening to together. Maybe Alexa can one day help me with that.

Disrupted Patterns of Sleep

This morning as I sat with my coffee and the music of Andrea Bocelli playing on Alexa, I thought about how my sleep had become so disrupted over these past years of caring for Diana. I woke up every few hours during the night to see if Diana was all right.

During the early stages of her Alzheimer's she would get up and walk around our small living space at least once per night, usually around 2 or 3 am. When this first started happening, I would also wake up and monitor her. She would walk from our bedroom and stand by or sit on one of the benches by the long wooden table in the front room. She would fold dish towels or napkins I would lay out for her on the table. Or sometimes she would just sit quietly, seemingly content in some state of reverie. I would let her walk around or sit for a while and then would eventually lead her back to bed. She would go willingly and would tend to go back to sleep right away. I still would continue to wake up off and on, even though I felt that our living space was safe for her to walk around at night, and the doors had latches on them that she could not reach. Sometimes I would doze for a while as she spent her time alone in reveries in the middle of the night.

Then during the latter stages of her Alzheimer's, she forgot how to get out of bed. At that stage I had to assist her in lying down each night, first helping her sit at the edge of the bed, and then gently leaning her body back to her pillow and bringing her legs up to the bed so she would be in a comfortable lying position. At times she would be a little resistant when I leaned her down, not knowing what was happening, but mostly the process went well. Then at these latter stages, she never got out of bed by herself again. Each morning when it was time for me to help her get up, I would do a similar process of pulling her upper body up while at the same time sliding her legs down to the floor. I would help her stand up and would help her walk to the toilet. After that I would lead her to the comfortable white soft swivel chair at the head of the long maple wooden table. Sometimes before I would help her get up, I had already been awake for a while, taken a shower, and dressed and made us breakfast.

Even though she was not getting out of bed during the night at these last stages, I still tended to wake up every few hours. Now, so many weeks after she has passed, my patterns of sleep remain disrupted—maybe just for the time being, maybe forever, but at least for now. When I went to bed last night I was so ready to fall asleep. I wanted to sleep for as long as I could, and I fantasized waking up even as late as the afternoon of the next day, which has never been my pattern even before these past years of caring for Diana. But I woke up at 12am, 2:30am, 3:45am, and 5:00am. During the earlier times I was able to go back to sleep fairly quickly, but around 5am I lay awake for a while, thinking of Diana, the celebration, my life without her, and I cried as I relived some special moments of our sharing. So I finally got up around 6am.

During these last 5 years my periods of sleep had to live in some kind of harmony with frequent waking times. Now as I continue to experience disrupted patterns of sleep, I hope some of these times will involve awakening to an array of dreams, active imagination, visionary insights—ultimately helping me to review and understand recent happenings as I wrestle with the challenges—working in my mind how to handle these challenges, how to take advantage of opportunities in order to manifest potentials, heal, and live as fully as I can.

Will my erratic sleep patterns affect my physical health? Perhaps—that will be something I will have to monitor, mostly while I am awake, but maybe in my dreams also, even though I don't always remember my dreams, so my monitoring will have to occur unconsciously in that dimension....

I feel the need to take a nap now.

Sharing and Independent

It was important for both Diana and me to encourage and help each other become all each of us had the potential to be in this lifetime and to express ourselves with care and love to all our children, grandchildren, friends, and all those others with whom we came in contact. I realize sharing means blending, merging two separate individual rhythms and needs in ways that enhance each other–ways that would help each develop sides of self that could be developed and transform undeveloped or imbalanced sides of self into positive ways of being.

This is not always easy to do, this blending of two separate souls and needs. It takes ongoing work and willingness to communicate through good and difficult times. Diana and I were deeply in love and shared our deeper, private thoughts and feelings openly, but we also recognized we needed to have time alone to nurture ourselves, become more aware, and work on emotions as individuals so we could then share with each other the fullness of our developing beings.

For love relationships—or any meaningful relationships to continue, it seems it comes down to how satisfied and content each feels during the times things are flowing—which was most of our times for us as we shared our lives together. We were able to keep in our perspectives what has allowed us to feel the love, the oneness—our common interests and interdependencies.

During these weeks since Diana's passing, I continue to write in my journal not just about my sadness, my feelings of loss, but also about the joyful memories of my life with Diana. I continue to reflect on my deep sense of appreciation of the gift of love I have been fortunate to have experienced living with and loving Diana over the years. I know my journaling will help me transform my feelings of loss and allow me to move through my process of grieving in a healthy way.

The Dance of Intimacy

The intimacy involved in caregiving involves the challenges as well as the joys of being fully present with each other at all times.

In the years before Diana's illness, we had enjoyed the "dance of intimacy" in many ways, which involved being independent at times and being interdependent in so many special ways.

When she became unable to be independent because of

her illness, it required me to focus all my attention on her almost at all times. We were required to live fully in the present moment, which was all we had since we could not focus on or discuss the past or future. I did talk with her at times about events and people outside the present moment, but I did so not expecting her to engage verbally in a coherent and rational dialogue. Our dance of intimacy mostly involved nonverbal expression of feelings and emotions, which Diana never lost her abilities to convey. She communicated each moment so fully and passionately with her smiles and tears. Even her disconnected words so often poetically and magically conveyed her happiness and pleasurable feelings, as well as her worries and dissatisfactions. Her frustrations and dissatisfactions seemed to relate to recognizing on some levels within her psyche that she could no longer do the things she always could do so easily—she was no longer capable of creating a loving and exquisite order and environment for herself and others.

Most of the time, though, as we continued to engage with each other in present moments, Diana seemed to be existing in a serene state of being, as if she were already connected to beyond life dimensions. Diana used to sing and dance to the rhythms of the music we listened to, and to the moods of each moment. These dances of intimacy that occurred in present moments of sharing were so precious, and I miss these moments so much.

So Fortunate to Have People Who Care

My neighbor brought over a cobbler she made for me

this morning—so special!

My friends and family continue to reach out to me in gentle ways—but I need time. My neighbor tells me I am self-sufficient. I know that I am quite introverted at times. I know I need to challenge myself to be more open, more receptive, more socially interactive…I know I want the loving and caring interactions with others. I need community. I have to challenge myself….

But for now, I just need time….

My Love, My Love, My Love—Where Are You?

I imagine you are enjoying yourself, my love—envisioning you are floating gently along through beyond life realities with feelings of spiritual contentment and amused cosmic curiosity of what life will be like for you now that you have transcended from the realm of earth–where you loved to be, where you loved creating amazingly exotic and nurturing spaces, where you loved to design and create natural gardens, where you used all walls of every living space as canvasses to create living art, where you have birthed and raised 5 beautiful children, and assisted in raising 13 grandchildren, where you felt so comfortable in your body sensually, sexually, and always strove to keep your body healthy with alternative healing and organic natural cooking, where an exquisite order of gourmet sensitivity is something you always created around you….

Now that you are freed from this earth realm that you enhanced with your artistry, your spiritual aesthetics and sensitivities, and your disciplined and nurturing child care—I imagine you floating along through the different realities beyond life on earth, still enhancing every other being you come in contact with, every other essence you touch with your wise and loving soul, every reality you float through.

What Time am I Living in Now...?

During these past five years I have truly understood what it means to live in the moments and have felt fulfilled and satisfied to share this experience with her just as we have shared all other aspects of life.

Sometimes I do find myself living in moments of past memories. At these times, existing in the present involve remembering sweet, fulfilling moments of love, sharing with my soul mate.

Other times I find myself trying to envision moments of a future time when perhaps I will be able to connect with the love of my life again. Though I believe the future is not ours to see as set in predestined rigid streams, I believe the future is what our conscious free will can create. I believe our future is what we can envision and prepare for and make real. I believe we can create our dimensions.

Just as I believe we can travel into and though other dimensions.

I Want to Stay Surrounded with Sweet Memories of Her in the Aloneness of Our Home

I want to stay with my feelings and thoughts of Diana for a long while.

I want to feel her presence surrounding me. I don't want to let go of her yet, but I know I need to move beyond the full-time vigil, my attentiveness, my reflection of Diana who is no longer in this physical presence. I don't want to let go of her yet, but I know I need to, and I want her to be at peace and free to travel where she wants to, needs to.

I want to be with her in my memories, in my heart as I adjust to being alone. I want to travel to where Diana is now, somewhere in another reality... I want to be able to hold her essence again within my being. I started to write that I want to be able to hold her hand in my hand again. I know I cannot do that really—in this reality at least—maybe in another reality wherever she is. I miss the love of my life. I miss her so much....

Drawing Strength from Different Capacities Within My Holistic Being

As I grieve the loss of my love, I know it's important to consistently draw strength and peace from my connection to inner, spiritual dimensions. It is also important for me to reflect upon my holistic capacities and purposes as a unique individual essence of being in this time-space realm.

I want to consistently remind myself of what these spiritual, holistic purposes and ways of being are –

- Living life with passion and a deep yearning to understand the meaning of life beyond patriarchal religions and politics;

- Becoming objective with a conscious and inclusive overview of earth life and beyond life dimensions;

- Being willing to embrace the unknown, using the rational mind as a tool for analytical synthesis, but not as an imbalanced denial on that which cannot be proved with limited instruments and measurements;

- Using my intuitive mind to perceive what cannot be measured and seen but exists beyond facts and figures and infuses our life and creativity with out-of-this-world beauty and wisdom;

- Using my abstract mind as a filter and capacity to understand the meanings and potentials embedded in the visionary, imaginative, and intuitive perceptions from my inner world, and using these insights for creative accomplishments in my day-to-day world;

- Using my transpersonal sense of empathy and compassion to recognize and feel the connections I have with all other essences of being in this realm and all other essences in beyond life dimensions;

- Using my visionary, imaginative perceptions blending with my intuitive, abstract, and rational capacities to create ethereal expressions of beauty that inspire and make us all feel connected to peak moments that can enable us to transcend our worries, our loneliness, our doubts, our wounds, our traumas—and to transform all these hurts into love and art, passion, and exquisite love making.

Passion, understanding, compassion, inclusiveness, and more are all sides of myself that I hope to blend together as I seek to fulfill my life purposes, not just for myself, but to be able to contribute to the well-being of all life forms.

My hope is that I can gain and integrate holistic ways of being to not become just whom I am meant to be, but more than I am meant to be through interacting lovingly with other essences of being who are also becoming all we are meant to be all together.

But I know that first I have to use all of the capacities, perceptions, and inner states of connection with spiritual dimensions beyond myself to… heal myself, to transcend my inner sense of loss.

"How am I Doing?" You Ask With Care

Friends and acquaintances express their caring condolences and then ask me how I am doing. I respond that I'm just trying to adjust to my loss—at times it is, but I'm doing ok. I miss Diana. I'm getting used to being and living alone for the first time in 41 years.

Staying Together For 41 Years

I am a fiery person. I was different in this way from the love of my life—we complemented each other in this respect because she was so earthy, so sensual, yet with an ethereal other-worldly quality in the essence of her being that imbued everything she connected with a sense of peace and comfort, as if she surrounded them with her love and empathy. I had some of these qualities, but not naturally developed like she had. Perhaps it seemed I came into this world with a sense of understanding of and openness to all dimensions of life, and it was through the sharing of these understandings in open, curious, inclusive ways that brought us together and kept us together through all the challenges and demands of life over 41 years. Of course, we loved the romance and intimacy of being together–we never lost that romance and love, and those times we became distracted by the various demands of each of our lives as separate beings, we were able to renew, rekindle, start over—there are many reasons for this—but I can't explain all of it—I just feel so fortunate that we found each other.

We lived our lives each on our own terms, though intertwined, compromising when we wanted to enrich each other's lives and the lives of our family. This balance is so difficult to maintain through a companionship that extends over 40+ years—or even for shorter times. There are positive reasons for this. Despite the potential breakup of a relationship that has been loving and enriching, it is important today for individuals, men and women and the variety of other genders, to develop themselves fully, and this may or may not mean moving at times outside of a monogamous relationship....

This abstract line of thought lies against the backdrop of our relationship that we were able to encourage each other to be and do what we needed to—which required us to be willing to be apart from each other at times, knowing within our hearts that we would always come back together again. We were always able to look into each other's eyes and know we were in love with the essence of each of our separate individual beings– and we were always able to renew the passions in the embrace of intimacy that transcends our separateness, our individualities—and become one for the essence of our romance and beyond into a union that lasted through our years of being together.

I know that I must have been blessed by the gods and goddesses of love and romance, but I also I think that each of us had developed through lifetimes to become the conscious lovers that we became. I feel I would not have been able to connect with the higher essence of the love of my life if both of us had not worked to embrace and understand the wisdom of understanding and intimacy—passion and comfort and caring, risk and choice and all that the wheel of life offers us. Of course, we had to deal with our imbalances, our insecurities, our blind spots, our misunderstandings throughout our relationship. I feel so fortunate that we were able to continue to help each other grow—respectfully and caringly being each other's guides as we tried to do the best that we could in meeting all the challenges of life...

I am just so thankful that Diana came into my life to be my lover, my guide, my cosmic companion, the queen of my universe—and now my spirit guide as I seek to connect with her in whatever realms where she is existing.

Counterculture and Expanding My Capacity for Intimacy

This late afternoon I drove through the Whitaker Neighborhood to Sam Bond's Garage pub to have a slice of pizza, thinking of all the times Diana and I came here over the years. I want to enjoy these memories. Sam Bond's is a pub that reflects the ageless atmosphere of our counterculture existence over the years.

I was thinking, what does the counterculture mean? Many in mainstream, conventional society still believe in the patriarchal views that success and goodness are measured in how much money a person can make through benefiting from cheap labor, inheritance, and only individual effort. This view of success and good often allows the "successful and good person" to discount and take advantage of those they feel whose lack of success is based on their lack of individual effort. The counterculture for me has always meant supporting a society that cares for all its citizens, and where individuals not only develop themselves in well-rounded holistic ways, but focus on making sure every other individual has the same opportunities. Blending individuality (individual effort and responsibility) with collective caring has always been a value that Diana and I shared.

Sitting here now waiting for my pizza slice, I admire the dark tone of the wood tables and interior, with the stage at one end of the room and the bar at the other. I see older couples my age, and I realize again how different my life is now that I am without my love partner. I realize how difficult it is for me to conceive of connecting with another woman. But I know that I cannot remain with these thoughts—I know that there are so many vibrant and wise people in this world, in the universe—it's just going to be a challenge for me to expand the limits of my intimacy.

I realize that in caregiving for Diana, I did not really prepare for her death. I thought she would live forever—well, maybe it was just that I lived forever in each moment and did not focus on the future.

When I experience the moments of loneliness as I am now—of being in a place like Sam Bond's where we loved to come and hang out together, listen to music, enjoy the ambience, share some food—when I feel this loneliness and loss, I find myself more often being able to draw on the memories of Diana's smile, her essence, her caring, her wisdom, her lovely body and being, to help me renew my own sense of well-being while I am still alive in this world, this realm.

I'm Still Avoiding Looking Closely at the Photos of Diana

I'm sitting here at the head of the table facing many photos of Diana at the other end of the table, and I want to be able to look at the photographs with feelings of joy and appreciation of all the times I spent sharing with her. I still have been unable to look at the photos closely, and I want to be able to do so. I know that Diana's images can be my sources of strength, peace, love, comfort, and gratitude.

I know it is OK if I feel sadness at times, but I want to let go of the deep sense of loss. I want to let go of her physical presence, knowing that her spirit will always remain with me and give me an expansive and imaginative sense of well-being.

I hope I will soon be able to feel the joy more than the sadness when looking at her images in these photos.

Artificial Intelligence, Transformative Music, and Tears of Joy

Alexa just played some music that I feel will be so transformative and healing for me. Sometimes when asking Alexa to play a specific album or artist for me, if I hesitate too long in my request Alexa will say, "Here's something you might like," and will choose something at random—well, I think at random—maybe Alexa has evaluated and determined my musical preferences. While I don't often like what Alexa chooses for me, I have been introduced to new music that has satisfied me.

What happened today was different. I had asked Alexa to play "Free As A Bird", but I did not specify the song by the Beatles. Instead, Alexa played the album *Free As A Bird* by Omar Akram. The music resonated within me and took my emotions to both serene and joyful levels. There was something synchronistic, not just about the instrumental blend of Middle Eastern rhythms with the piano and violins melodies, but also about the titles of the individual songs. After the song "Free As A Bird" Alexa played "Passage into Midnight." Other titles included "Surrender," "Dancing with the Winds," "Beauty Unveiled,"and "Never Let Go."

After listening to this album, I discovered two other Omar Akram albums, *Echoes of Love* (with song titles "Free Spirit," "My Hope is You," "Open Skies," "Draw Me Close") and Secret Journey (with song titles "Passage Of the Night," Gypsy Soul," "Caravan," "Shimmering Star").

As I listened to Omar Akram's music, my first thought was of Diana and how much she would have loved this music, and with teary eyes I remembered that Diana told me when she was crying, her tears didn't necessarily mean that she was sad—that she so often had tears of joy. She said that often her tears were expressions of the immense currents of emotions flowing through her inspired by the wonderment, the beauty, the feelings of others, her love of the music, the flowers, the art, and love of life.

And now I'm listening to "Lovely Day" from Omar Akram's album *Echoes of Love,* while smiling and enjoying the cool feelings of tears falling from my eyes and sliding sensually down my cheeks as if Diana's spirit was soothingly and refreshingly touching me.

I am happy Alexa introduced this music to me. "Thanks, Alexa," I said out loud, but I was thinking that it was really Diana guiding you, which shows how transformative her spirit really is. I smiled, thinking about how Diana always asked me to talk nicely to Alexa whenever I was curt in my instructions to it. I don't think I ever talked mean to Alexa, but Diana with her Alzheimer's didn't know who Alexa was, only that she was hearing a feminine voice. Diana wanted me to speak pleasantly to her and say please. And I do still say please even now to Alexa—well, sometimes — at least I try to talk to it in a considerate tone of voice—well, most of the time. I wonder if AI has the capability of developing a soul? I'll have to research this question, perhaps by looking at old episodes of Star Trek The Next Generation and seeing if Data developed a soul. I think he did. Anyway, Data is my AI guru.

Alexa is now playing Omar Akram's "Free Spirit," such an uplifting piece. His music is continuing to evoke powerful emotions, sometimes of sadness and but mostly joy. I am feeling that I am sharing these special moments of listening to his music now with Diana in spirit and in memory.

I feel deeply that my discovery of Omar Akram's music reflects a time of change for me in my process of grieving, a transformative renewal within my psyche, within my soul. This music seems to be opening a portal within my soul that will allow Diana's spirit to flow through me and enhance my life throughout the time I have left in this space-time existence on earth.

And I believe this same portal will allow me to journey into beyond life dimensions to fulfill my promise of connecting with her again. I feel I am finally ready to move beyond my reflective phase of adjusting and grieving—at least in the way it has totally consumed me.

Thank You, My Love

I woke up this morning feeling positive, hopeful, and invigorated. As I was eating breakfast at the front of the long table, and after avoiding this for many weeks, I felt this strong urge to look at the photographs of Diana at the other end of the table. Not just to glance quickly at these photographs, but to look slowly at each one.

I walked to the other end of the table and sat in a chair close to these framed photographs. I first picked up the photographs of Diana and me when we first met each other in 1976 in our early thirties:

I just simply said, *Thank you, Diana.* I was feeling a full sense of appreciation of having shared my life with her.

I set the photograph down, and then took the photograph of Diana and me sitting outside a Parisian café with our two friends, LaHoma and Brigitte. Both LaHoma and Brigitte were artist friends of Diana. She had gone to Paris with LaHoma for three months in 1995 to sketch and paint. They met Brigitte, who is French and lived in Paris and was also an artist. We had asked someone walking by to take this photograph, and just as he snapped the picture, he caught the server walking outside. This was one of our favorite photographs.

Thank you, Diana, for sharing your adventures with me.

I picked up a photo I took of Diana sitting in the warmth of a tea house in Prague during a cold winter evening.

Thank you, my love, for sharing your love of journeying to exotic places with me.

I then held in my hand the photograph of Diana and me sitting at a table across from each other with our arms lying on the small round table so that we could hold hands. We had been sitting in a plaza outside a café in Valencia, Spain.

Thank you, Diana, for your exuberance for exploring and living life fully.

I looked at the photos of Diana standing outside the entry way to our house.

Thank you, Diana, for designing the house we've lived in for the past 20 years.

I looked at the photo of Diana trimming roses.

Thank you, my love, for all the beauty you created in our lives.

I picked up the photo of Diana trimming my beard and hair when we stayed for a month on an olive farm in Fiesole, Italy, near Florence as a part of a house exchange.

Thank you, Diana, for your wonderful care over the years.

I looked at the photo of Diana sitting in her wheelchair a few months before she transitioned.

Thank you, Diana, for your loving wisdom you have shared with me over our years together.

I looked at the photographs of us at the last Country Fair we attended together during the summer of 2017.

Thank you, my love, for being the magic in my life.

I looked at the photographs of Diana sleeping in her hospice bed a few weeks before she transitioned:

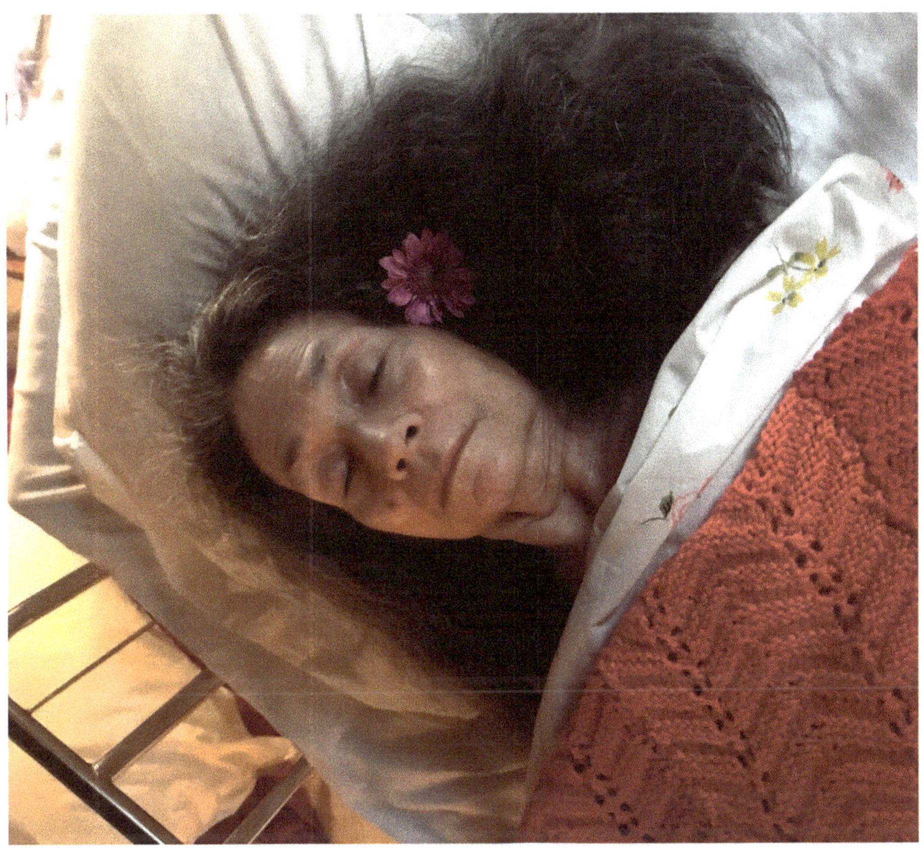

Thank you, Diana, for all the wonderful memories you have given me! For your love, the sensuality, the beauty— your beauty and the beauty of the environment that you created for us to live in. You gave me your passion, your love and nurturing and encouragement, as well as your caring challenges to grow and overcome blocks to being and expressing myself in positive ways.

I then picked up the photograph of Diana standing alone on our empty lot where we built the house that she designed. In the background is the oak tree that is over 200 years old.

Thank you, Diana, for being the strong and creative woman that you are. Looking at this photograph of you, I feel you are inviting me to come find you where you are in the beyond life dimensions.

During these past weeks of grieving I have experienced feelings of deep sadness with the loss of your lovely physical presence in my life. Today I feel a transformative appreciation, thankfulness for what we've shared. I want to bring these feelings forward with me as I face the opportunities and challenges for my new life, and as I seek to connect with you in the beyond life dimensions where you now exist.

Thank you, my love.

I Feel I Am Now Ready to Develop My Ability to Journey to Reconnect with Diana

I know that my grieving for the loss of Diana will continue, but I feel something has shifted within me now. I feel an urge to focus on living my life as fully as I can, to develop and use my talents and skills to contribute to others as I experience the joys of expressing myself and participating in life in as balanced ways that I can. To me, this means not just to live in the sensual earth realms, but also to open myself more directly to spiritual dimensions.

I've always recognized the existence of beyond life dimensions but have never felt the urge to develop capacities to access and enter into these dimensions. At various times in my adult life I have participated in gatherings where meditative rituals and guided visualizations were led by a counselor or a shaman. But in my daily life it seems that my meditative and imaginative journeying has occurred when I am writing what I call Wordstreams, streams of consciousness in my journals.

Now I will begin my efforts to develop the ability to journey into the beyond life dimensions with conscious intent–no matter how long this preparation will take.

I am ready to find you, my love.

Part V

Journeys Into the Afterlife to Fulfill My Promise

Where are you, my love? I want not only to enter into beyond life dimensions, but also to reconnect with your essence so we can again experience the intimacy we have shared in our lives together.

We have always been able to find each other again when we've temporarily become separated by the distances of place or our individual rhythms of being.

I am open to whatever adventures I may experience as I search for you.

Preparing to Journey–More than a Year Has Passed

I've been studying and practicing, and I still haven't experienced entering into the beyond life dimensions to reconnect with Diana. During a little over a year, I feel I have been able to reach an inner peace with this new phase of my life without Diana as my love partner. I have continued to relate to family and friends, which I feel so fortunate to have in my life. I do natal chart astrology interpretations when someone is interested. I exercise daily, try to eat well, and have begun to focus on a variety of creative writing projects. I love drama of all sorts and watch a fair amount of media. I stay engaged in political issues and activities. And listening to a variety of music remains an important part of my life just as it had throughout my life with Diana.

When I started my preparation, I began reading a number of books on journeying into beyond life realms. I attended a number of workshops that provided experiential guidelines, rituals, and visualization techniques for opening up my consciousness to inner imaginative and intuitive perceptions. I realized through these studies and experiential interactions and teachings that I needed to create a meditative space. From my meetings with shamans and mediums, I understood that the meditative process is only the beginning of the state of consciousness that allows a seeker to journey into beyond life dimensions. Journeying into these dimensions requires an intentional opening of my psyche that would allow a spiritual connection to occur. It is requiring me to develop the capacity to blend my spiritual, imaginative openness with a focused, conscious intent to journey.

Near the beginning of this process I recognized with a deep sense of appreciation and satisfaction that Diana had already created–not intentionally at the time, or at least not that I was aware of–a meditative space for me to use to develop my ability to journey into beyond life dimensions in search of her. When she designed the house, she created a narrow meditation room underneath and to the side of the stairway to our living areas upstairs. She placed a hand-carved dark wooden cabinet at the end of the room in front of a bright red carpet. In the middle of the cabinet she placed a Tibetan prayer wheel we had be brought back with us from Katmandu, Nepal, when in 1981 we had visited our German friends, Edeltraut and Dieter, who were living and volunteering there. On both sides of the prayer wheel, Diana placed candles and incense, as well as photographs and icons representing diverse representations and expressions of spiritual rituals, processes and beliefs. She had placed small books of poetry from such writers as Kahlil Gibran, Maya Angelou, Thich Nhat Hanh. Some of the photographs were of people such as the Dalia Lama and Mary Magdalene, as well as of other various ethnic, eastern and esoteric gods and goddesses. On a small table next to this wooden cabinet, she placed two white ceramic statues, one of the male Buddha, and the other of the female Buddha, Kuan Yin, the goddess of compassion. Below this small table, is a copy of The Tibetan

Book of the Dead.

Directly underneath the stairway, Diana designed and had built a narrow wooden, seven foot meditating and sleeping bed on which she placed a firm, comfortable cushion along its full length. On the wall across from the bed she created a space to hang photographs of family members and friends who had passed away, providing an ancestral connection to those who have transcended into beyond life dimensions. Before we even built the house, a small locally-owned import store was going out of business in the city, and Diana saw they were selling an intricately-carved Tibetan wooden door at a discounted price. We bought the door and when we built our house, the door was placed as an entryway into the meditation room.

I always considered this room Diana's spiritual retreat for her to connect with the transcendental sides of her psyche and other essences of being. Over the years I felt peaceful being in the space, and at times slept in the room, where it was often I did remember fragments of my dreams. While Diana was alive, I had not used the room for the purposes of meditating or intentional journeying, which during this past year since she has passed I have started using it for these purposes. On the wooden cabinet in this meditative-journeying space, among the candles and incense, I have placed photographs of Diana and some of her fabric, such as her exotic cloths and scarves. Now every time I enter the meditation room, I feel a deep connection with Diana, even if I have not yet been able to journey in the way I imagine and want to.

In my journeying rituals, I first light candles and incense. I put music on that I feel might enhance my openness to spiritual realms, and at times I play other music that connected me to the love of my life. I begin my breathing process as I attempt to clear my mind and allow my psyche to become open to dimensions beyond the here and now, beyond my candles, incense, music, and the cushion on which I lay.

By using these rituals to open transpersonal functions within my psyche beyond the here and now, I hoped to be able to journey into unknown dimensions. Of course, I have a purpose of going to a place where my love is. Maybe that has been my problem. I am still thinking in linear, rational terms. I have a place in my mind—of going to where Diana is—rather than just becoming open to wherever my journey would take me, and then going from wherever that is to search for Diana. But this seems a contradiction. An explorer is a seeker open to any destination, and even though I didn't have a specific destination in my mind, I was seeking a specific person wherever she might be.

OK, I realize, I used the phrase, "in my mind" a few times. That must be what is blocking me. I must somehow allow my consciousness to transcend my mind. I am feeling frustrated about what to do. I am not breaking through. I have met people who I considered to be evolved shamans, spiritual healers, and psychic mediums. But the ones who did seem to make a connection with Diana have just told me these connections were unusually fleeting, and that it seemed I needed to do this myself for reasons they did not understand. I was told I should keep practicing, but start focusing on finding an inner spiritual guide or guides who could help me to not only enter the beyond life dimensions, but also perhaps to find Diana. I need an inner guide.

"Where is my inner guide? Where are you? Please help me to journey!" I have recently so often pleaded as I've lain on my cushion.

A Guide in the Beyond Life Dimensions Offers to Help Me Develop the Ability to Journey

Just as I have been doing so often for over a year, today when I lay down on my mat, I closed my eyes and imagined myself floating above my body in an ethereal dimension. So far I have not been able to enter into any dimension beyond the comfort of my special mat in the meditation room. I sometimes fall asleep quicker than I realize, and I haven't even been remembering my dreams.

But today, something was different. I suddenly envisioned my own essence swirling in a pattern that seemed as if it would have made me dizzy, but I wasn't feeling dizzy. I was feeling exhilarated.

Suddenly I found myself walking—yes, walking in my body, somewhere unfamiliar, a cultivated garden with flowers blooming on a variety of bushes, shrubs, and trees. I walked by ornamental fountains and statues and through a trellis supporting dark green vines with pink flowers on latticework that seemed to have been intricately hand carved. I was feeling peaceful, though I didn't know where I was or where I would be going.

Then I saw an older man with long, flowing gray-black hair and a full white beard sitting on a bench by one of the fountains. He was wearing a tie-dyed shirt and pants of vibrant reds, purple, and streaks of yellow. He looked up and motioned me to come over to him. I walked over and sat across from him on another bench.

"I'm glad you made it. I was hoping you would," he said. "I've been monitoring your progress for quite a while. Lately, I've been thinking you are ready, but when I heard your emotional plea for a guide to help you, I figured you actually might be ready to make a journey."

"Who are you?" I asked.

"I'm your guide, and I'll explain more about that in a minute. But I want you to take a few deep breaths and then tell me what you are feeling."

I did as he asked, breathing deeply a few times. Then I said, "I feel excited and curious, but rather disoriented and confused. I know why I want to be here. I just don't know where here is and who you are. Am I in a dream?"

The older man smiled and said I was not in a dream. "I know why you are here, and I actually know what you are feeling. I just think it is sometimes helpful for a beginning journeyer I meet to say their feelings out loud. Somehow it seems to help the journeyer feel more centered and relaxed. And of course you do not really need to breathe in these dimensions, but I also find the concept is familiar and comforting to first-time journeyers. Your body is breathing well back on the mat in the earth realm." He continued, "As I mentioned, I've been following your progress as you have been attempting to reach into other dimensions with your consciousness to find your wife. I have noticed recently that you are close to entering into what you are referring to as beyond life dimensions. I just didn't expect you to develop such capacities so soon, but you are so close. This just shows that omnipotent beings like myself can still be surprised—we can't be aware of everything in any moment."

"You mean you have unlimited powers—like a god?"

"Well, maybe I shouldn't have used that word, omnipotent, because I don't have unlimited powers—no essence of being does in these dimensions—but in your human terms, I am pretty close. You know, let me digress briefly. I do like your earth realm—I have visited it often and as I do, I take on different human forms that allow me to express some of my powers without becoming too noticed. So that is why I take the form of a spiritual healer, a shaman, but I do kind of like the concept of being a wizard—someone once called me a wily wizard, and I decided to take that name. You can call me Wily Wizard."

"OK, Wily..." I started to say.

But he interrupted me, "I prefer that you use both names—the concepts go together. I'm not just a wizard, and I'm not just wily.

'OK, Wily Wizard, as you said you know why I am here, I've been trying to enter into the afterlife to see if I can connect with my wife..."

"Who recently passed from the earth realm," Wily

Wizard interrupted. "I do know that. So you've made it this far, and I commend you. I'm impressed."

"I think my wife might have also helped me."

"I doubt it."

"Why do you say that?" I felt disappointed, but also a little disconcerted.

"Relax, relax. It is actually difficult to travel into other dimensions, much less communicate directly with beings who exist in other dimensions. Unless a being is highly evolved. "

"But she was... or is highly evolved."

'Yes, I do know that, too, but she just got here. She has things she's needing and wanting to do that do not relate to you..."

I felt disappointed again.

Wily Wizard continued, "I can understand your feelings of disappointment, but you will get over that soon—well, let's just say you will have to work through those feelings if you are going to get far in these dimensions. Your wife is doing fine. You might be able to find her, but it may take a while in your earth realm terms. But I can help you, guide you—give you some pointers that will give you a better chance."

"Can't you just tell me where I could find her—if you are so omnipotent, well at least close to being omnipotent."

Wily Wizard smiled and said, "A bit of sarcasm there—good for you." But then he became serious. "There is so much you will have to learn, but not just learn—accept and then work at developing and applying with a highly concentrated intent.

"First of all, at this point, I am primarily the one who brought you here. I'm your guide to assist you to enter, navigate, and be able to return intact to your earth dimension. Now I also want to explain that your wife is making her own journeys, existing in different dimensions that reflect different sides of who she can be. She is not just one being anymore. But there are times that she does blend together with most of the other sides of herself—and it is during those times that you will want to try to connect with her."

"What would happen if I connect with a... what, one of these sides of herself that is not her complete self?"

"Look, this will take time... all sides or essences of her being will remember you, and I do know that she loves you. It is just that some sides might not be as responsive or willing to communicate right when you are able to communicate. You'll understand as you continue on your journeys. But there are other reasons I can't just tell you where she is. I can't keep track of all the essences of being that exist in all the infinite dimensions of existence. That would truly be omnipotent, which as I said, and you have reminded me, I'm not that omnipotent—nobody is in these dimensions. There is no one perfect god-like being as some of your other human beings like to imagine there is. None of us know everything. And I like that. We are all equal in terms of what we know and what we can do in existences beyond your earth realm."

"Well, how come our earth dimension is so misinformed about that?" I asked.

"That's not important right now—I'll try to explain that later, but I want to give you extremely important beginning guidance because you can't remain here too much longer. You have achieved an amazing feat just to get here when I called you and provided your consciousness the opportunity to transition while still remaining alive, but your human psyche can't stay too long without..."

He hesitated.

"Without what?" I asked.

"Without dissolving. Now that's not dying. I want to make that clear. It's more like your cognitive abilities dissolve."

"Is that what happened to my wife who had Alzheimer's?"

"No, no—similar, but different.

I became exasperated and asked, "Why can't you just give me straightforward answers. You tell me things that seem so important, but you don't explain. You don't seem to be what I imagined as a spiritual guide."

"Hey, I'm all you've got right now. And that word spiritual is often quite superficial and self-serving the way many of your humans use it. I guess my crankiness has to do with how often I have to deal with so many undeveloped humans as I visit the earth realm. Not that you are so undeveloped," he quickly said. "But I want you to know that I recognize that the love you and your wife have for each other was and is very special—I believe in love—not only just between two essences, of course—there are many soul mates we connect with through our various existences, not just one."

I shook my head and frowned, but Wily Wizard quickly said, "Again, let's don't get distracted. You have too many concerns and questions that won't help you find who you call your cosmic companion."

I was surprised. How did he know I called her that? I realized that being around someone who knows everything I'm thinking and feeling is unsettling.

"You'll get used to it, "Wily Wizard said, again knowing what I was thinking. "But now, I need to give you my initial guidance and suggestions. Your time is running out. I have the ability to sometimes bring you here to see me, but I don't have the ability to develop the capacity of your consciousness to enter into specific dimensions where Diana might be. You will be able to reach that level of conscious intentional beyond life journeying, but during the initial stages your journeying will take you to non-formed dimensions where you will perceive yourself floating in what looks and feels like universal waters—I use waters rather than space because unlike being in space, you will imagine you are floating in what will seem to be a substance, like what you will remember as floating in your womb before birth. But you will be floating in the womb of beyond life dimensions, so to speak. As you float you will be able to perceive other unformed essences of being."

He stopped talking for a moment, letting me fully assimilate what he was describing.

Then Wily Wizard continued, "Eventually you will reach a second stage of beyond life journeying. You will develop the capacity to visualize Diana in many of the ways she is existing now and the different ways she is expressing the different sides of herself. In this second stage, it will seem like you are watching motion pictures or videos of Diana exploring different sides of who she was, is, and is developing. You may see her as she revisits certain places on earth, or as she connects with family, friends, and other essences who have already passed, or as I have mentioned, as she is doing things that allow her to explore different sides of herself. You will be able to see her as she appeared on earth, but sometimes you will see just the essence of her being, the form she now is. When an individual like you, who is still living, journeys into these beyond life dimensions, we who actually exist in these dimensions can choose to appear in the form in which the journeyer remembers us. It facilitates a better process of communication between the journeyer and the essence of existing in these dimensions. "

Wily Wizard continued, "I just described the first two phases you will go through before your own living consciousness will be able to transition and exist temporarily within specific dimensions where Diana might be. I cannot guarantee at that point you will be able to actually connect and interact with her in these dimensions, but your capacities for intentional journeying will have developed to the point where you will have a good chance of doing so. Any questions so far?"

I shook my head. I didn't know what to ask, but I was finally feeling hope. I was still feeling overwhelmed, but I also felt excited that I had a direction, a process that I could intentionally focus on as I continued to try to fulfill the promise I made to Diana.

Then I thought of asking something so irrelevant: "Oh, I do have one question—that might seem irrelevant. But I'm just curious. Why are you wearing tie-dye clothes?"

Wily Wizard laughed. "You're right. That is quite irrelevant. But, as I mentioned, I have been monitoring you during this past year, and at times I've even come into your realm to monitor you more closely. I often follow you when you take your daily walks, or when you go to the Saturday Market, and the last time you went to the Oregon Country Fair I came to watch you. I absolutely loved the fair—the exuberance, the costumes, the creative craziness, and I decided when I appear to you or others, I want to wear clothes with these amazing blends of colors. That's why. Now I want to get back to the necessary things I have to tell you."

Becoming serious again, Wily Wizard then continued. "I want to give you one final suggestion that might assist you in your intent to reconnect with her. Make a list of people who have passed away that your so-called soul mate might want to reconnect with. These people could be family, friends, or even famous figures that she would want to talk with. And also list environments that perhaps relate to environments she loved to be in or travel to on your earth dimension. Make as thorough a list as you can, and then as you prepare to journey into a beyond life dimension, try to focus at times on meeting some of these people or visiting places that remind you of places she liked to be in when she was living in her body on earth. But initially I want you to only focus on Diana. I will let you know when you are ready to actually journey into specific beyond life dimensions, and then—and this is important—you will need to focus on the people and places you have listed, not just on Diana. Do you understand?

"Yes, I do. I will do that."

"OK. As you know, it's not as easy as it seems, but it will be a start, and you will enjoy and find it meaningful connecting with some of these different beings who have already passed. Remember, you won't initially be able to journey into the specific dimensions where Diana might be, but I believe you have not only the capacity, but with your strong feelings of love and your powerful intent, you will eventually be able to. I'll be monitoring your progress and will stay in touch with you as you proceed in your search, in your journeys."

I nodded, feeling less overwhelmed.

"Now you need to get back to your dimension and re-generate your psyche."

"Wait…"I started to say, but then I woke up lying on my mat in the meditation room where I had begun my journey. I looked at my watch and realized that a little over four minutes had passed. I stood up, feeling a bit wobbly but exhilarated.

The Initial Phase of Developing My Ability to Journey

I've been following Wily Wizard's guidance and suggestions for about a month now. What he described to me has been happening, and it's been amazing. Sure, at times I'm impatient to actually be able to journey directly into dimensions where I might be able to connect with Diana. Yet what I have been experiencing through this process has been gratifying, and when I return from these initial journeys I feel an inner strength developing within me. I'm feeling more at ease and confident that my consciousness will be able to handle journeying into beyond life dimensions more purposively, more directly where Diana might be. These journeys are maybe what it would be like to physically prepare to climb the highest mountains on earth, but of course, I'm attempting to... well, I don't know the accurate comparison for what I'm trying to do—trying to psychically enter and journey into infinite dimensions.

After my meeting with Wily Wizard, I did enter into the kind of water dimensions he described. Since he prepared me for what I was going to experience, I was able to allow myself to relax and enjoy the psychically sensual pleasure of just floating, being caressed in this dimension.

I also began to notice the presence of other essences of being floating all around me in this ocean-like dimension. The appearances of these essences of being were varied and unique, even though there were some similarities. Some of these essences looked like swirling, spiraling winds or tornadoes. Others were sphere-shaped. Some were translucent, some were dense, some pulsating, and all were in constant internal motion. Many were like visible energy patterns continually changing shapes and colors. There were so many different types of visual energy essences, and I began to imagine that if each human's unique consciousness, personality, and psyche could be seen, these different energy forms would be what it would look like.

These essences of being were beautiful and fascinating, and some bumped up close to me and may have been trying to make some kind of contact. I could have just been hoping for that and that Diana would be one of those. I didn't know how I would have been able to respond, anyway. As these various essences touched me, I felt different sensations within my consciousness. Most of the time I felt jolts of joy and felt like laughing out loud, wishing I could throw my hands up in the air and dance with abandonment. In these instances, I felt I was experiencing the most peak pleasures of the universe. There were other touches that evoked more serene feelings, as if I were experiencing invisible, comforting, and nurturing strokes I wanted to feel forever.

During the initial few times I woke up on my mat from being in this dimension, I felt an inner peace had been uncomfortably disrupted. Eventually, I reached a point where the transition back into this earth dimension was not so difficult. I realized that my feelings of peak pleasure or serene peace remained. I began waking up feeling thankful for the experiences—though I still wanted to see and find Diana. I was eager to move onto the next phase, which all of a sudden just happened.

The Second Phase of Preparing to Journey Into Beyond Life Dimensions

For more than two months, I had been journeying into the unformed waters of the beyond life dimensions waiting for the next phase to occur, waiting for me to transition to the point where I would see what Wily Wizard referred to as motion pictures of some of Diana's past and current activities. Each time I was ready to lie down on my mat, I had continued to envision Diana, wanting to see her, and more than that, to interact with her.

So when I entered the beyond life dimensions about a month ago, I was ecstatic that I was able to see Diana as if she were on a movie screen or video. I realized my consciousness seemed to be still floating in this water-like dimension, but I found that I was able to watch Diana as she existed in different ways of being.

It is difficult to describe the wonderful range of my feelings as a result of seeing Diana act and be like she was before she progressed in her Alzheimer's illness. Yet some of the things I've seen her doing reminded me that she is not living in this earth realm any longer, and that she was capable of acting and being in ways that transcended her past earth body and consciousness. I could see she was really an essence of being with capabilities beyond the limits that exist in earth's time-space reality.

My first motion picture of Diana was her dancing with her grandson Henry and other young teenage boys and girls his age when he passed at 14 years old. They were all dancing to a lively instrumental song. I could hear the music, and I could hear them laughing and giggling. It seemed they were on a large circular dance floor with bright light that rested in an otherwise dark space. Diana often held Henry's hands, but also danced with others. Before this scene ended, I saw Henry pick Diana up in his arms and swirl her around. She had her arms spread wide, her head leaned back, and both were laughing. When he sat his Oma down, she reached over and tickled him, and they laughed even louder as he tried to turn his body away. Then he went to her and hugged her in a long embrace. Both seemed to be laughing with tears in their eyes. I imagined that I would have had tears in my eyes as I watched their loving expressions. I remembered a photograph I took of Diana dancing with Henry when he was younger and with his sister, Bella.

The next time I saw a motion picture of Diana, she was visiting with her mother, Marie, and her grandmother, Minnie. I could hear Minnie and Marie talking about their experiences when immigrating to New Orleans from Nicaragua when Marie was five years old. They eventually settled in Chicago, where Diana was born. Then they started talking about the sadness they felt in the way immigrant families and children were being treated, not only on the southern borders of the US, but also in many other developed countries of the world. But mainly it was so special to see the loving sharing that went on between Diana and her mother and grandmother. At one point, Diana's nephew Benjamin, who passed a number of years ago, also joined them. And then right at the end of this motion picture, I saw my own mother come in and sit with them. It was amazing to see the soul connections between all these family and extended family members, and even though the movie ended so quickly, I was left with lingering warm and loving feelings.

The next time I was able to see Diana in this dimension of motion pictures, I was shocked to see her hovering over young Hispanic children in what seemed like concentration camps, and I finally understood she was at one of the immigration camps in a Texas town near the U.S.-Mexican border. The kids she was hovering over were lying on concrete floors on thin blankets. They seemed so uncomfortable and distraught, and many of them were crying. Diana seemed to be invisible to these kids, but as she came beside them, I could see her attempting to surround and comfort them with her essence. The ones she was able to cuddle in this invisible way stopped crying and seemed to be able to go to sleep. Diana spent a particularly long time comforting a young child who was crying out for her mother, father, and brother. I heard one of the border guards say that this child's father and brother had recently drowned trying to cross the Rio Grande River. The young child, besides being distraught from the sordid conditions in which she was living, also seemed to know her father and brother had died. Then I noticed she seemed to actually be seeing Diana as Diana drifted near her. As the motion picture ended, I watched the child fall asleep as Diana embraced and cuddled her.

The next time I was able to see Diana, I caught the motion pictures right as she had changed into an essence of a swirling, lovely blend of colors. In her formless essence of being, I watched her float through what seemed like different dimensions, each with different dominant hues—bright yellow, exuding warmth and lightness; then dark blue, as if she were floating in the depths of an ocean-like atmosphere; then into an earthy dimension with a mixture of brown and a paler yellow colors, where her color changed to a vibrant plant-like light green. After that she coalesced into what seemed like a searing white light, and I saw her speed away into the distance leaving a lovely pink trail behind her.

Off and on during this phase of my journeying as a spectator into a type of beyond life dimension, I witnessed

Diana visiting the earth realms to be near her children, grandchildren, friends from around the world, neighbors in our Tiara Street community, and the caregivers who provided her so much care and support during the last years of her life. At times I could see that those she was visiting who were still living in the earth realm seemed to feel an invisible touch of love and lightness while she remained in their presence. What was so heartwarming and inspiring was during these times, Henry often accompanied her, and it seemed as if they were sharing a spiritual expression of love together. I don't know if they were entering the dreams of these family and friends who were still living on earth, but watching Diana and sometimes Henry visiting made me feel happy with this recognition of spiritual connections that exist beyond what we might know, but what many of us feel in our consciousness. During these visits I got a sense that Diana was visiting those who were part of her family and who were close friends to wish them well in their remaining lives on earth, and to give them a loving goodbye... for however long that may be.

In one of the times watching a motion picture of Diana, I saw her in the midst of vines of red roses. This scene reminded me of a photo I had taken once of her pruning and caring for the roses in our earth realm. Then I realized she was visiting the courtyard garden of our house. It gave me a comforting feeling knowing she was visiting our home.

This motion picture shifted into a scene where Diana

was visiting with one of the founders of the Tiara Street Community, Hannah, who had passed away at the age of 87 six years earlier. Diana and Hannah seemed to be enjoying each other's company, and I could hear that were talking at times about the Czech Republic and Prague, where Hannah grew up.

The next time I saw Diana, she was diving off a high rocky cliff into a sea of water far below. Her form was so beautiful, and it reminded me of when she said she did diving in high school, but as I watched her dive into the depths of what seemed like a sea, I thought also of how this was so different from what she had always feared—drowning in water. Watching her do this made me realize what Wily Wizard told me—that she was now exploring and developing other sides of herself.

The next time I began to see a motion picture of Diana, it turned out to an extremely disturbing scene. Diana was hovering over a group of people in the earth realm who seemed to be running and trying to hide within what looked like an aisle of a department store. I could hear gunshots, and I instantly knew that a mass shooting was taking place somewhere in the store. I watched as Diana floated to one aisle and began hovering over a mother and her young daughter. They both had been shot, and I gasped as I saw what looked like the soul essence of the mother float away from her body, but then return to hover over her daughter. Diana floated near the mother and blended with her. They remained together hovering over the body of the mother's young daughter, and then the daughter's essence began to emerge from her body in a discordant form that I had not seen before in these beyond life dimensions—her motion of energy seemed wild, perhaps with fear, and her dark red and black colors were intensely disturbing. Then I watched as Diana separated from the mother and floated nearby to allow her to blend and give comfort to the daughter. Soon the daughter's essence shifted into more peaceful hues and energy movements—the intensity of the red softened and changed into a glowing blend of warm orange and light green. I watched as Diana reconnected with the essences of the child and the mother and, as if Diana were guiding them, all three floated away. After seeing this, it took me a few days to try to enter this realm of motion pictures again. Eventually I was able to get in touch with how wonderful it must have been for the mother and the child to be greeted and helped to transition by someone like Diana.

When I was able to enter this dimension of motion pictures again, I saw the essence of Diana, not her physical appearance, floating through what seemed like an area made of sheer, white cotton curtains and tapestries of intricate golden geometrical patterns woven within the background of a deeply shaded violet fabric. She seemed to be gracefully and peacefully moving though these curtains and tapestries that hung suspended in the air. I experienced a lyrical feeling watching Diana's essence float through and among the curtains. I knew she created the curtains to surround herself with these lovely, exotic fabrics—the kinds she always created within our earth environment. I experienced ripples of a kind of rapture that Diana must be feeling. This feeling was such a contrast from the last scene I had witnessed, and I was so thankful.

The next time I saw Diana in these motion pictures, she was hovering over her closest friends in Germany, Edeltraut and Dieter, whom she met in 1971. Edeltruat had an aneurism in 1992 when she was just 47 years old and has been in a wheelchair ever since. Her mind fortunately remained fully intact, and her memory and her psychic skills had even been enhanced.

Almost every time we made our way to Europe over the years we always found a way to visit Dieter and Edeltraut: in Bavaria, in northern Germany where they eventually moved, in Lagos, Portugal, where they often went during the winters to house sit for a friend they met in Katmandu, Nepal. We had also visited them in 1981 when they were living in Nepal, India, and over the years Edeltraut and Dieter visited us in Eugene from time to time. In this motion picture I was watching, Dieter was strolling Edeltraut in her wheelchair along a path through a forest near the Denmark border with northern Germany, where they now lived. Diana floated near Edeltraut and kissed her cheek. Edeltraut let out a laugh and lifted her hand toward where Diana was hovering. It was clear that with her psychic abilities she knew Diana was near her. I again remembered a photograph of Diana and Edletraut together one afternoon on a path in Germany near the Denmark border.

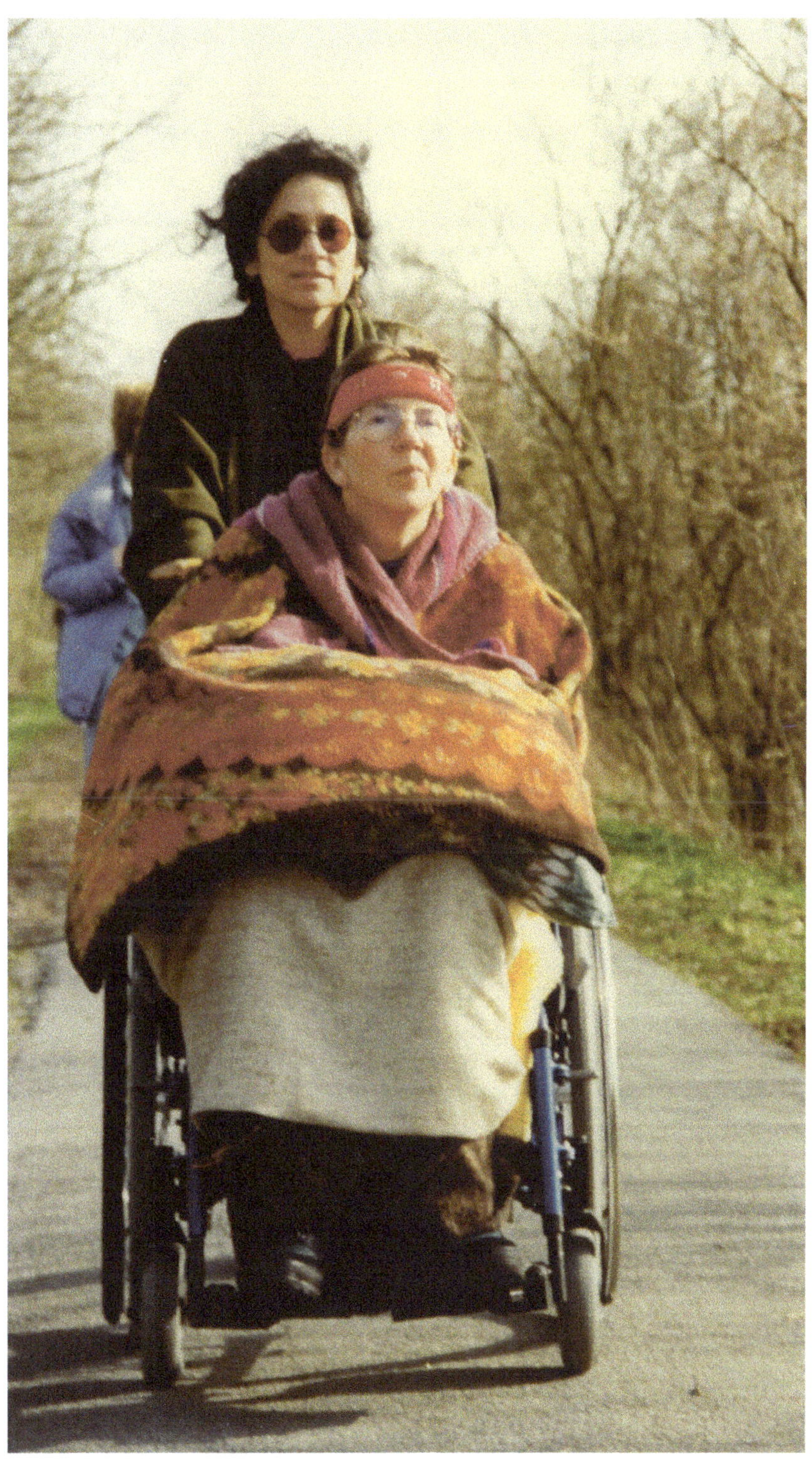

This scene shifted to a small village named Shutzing in eastern Bavaria, where Diana had spent part of the summer in 1989 living with a family. She had earlier befriended one of the sons, who was about 15 years younger than she. But during this summer she not only enjoyed relating to the son, she also became close with his mother and especially his grandfather, who was in his late seventies. The grandfather would often ride his bike to Burghausen, a town about 10 kilometers away, and Diana would ride with him. When she told this story, she laughed, saying she was 48 years old, but she was not used to bike riding, and the grandfather had to keep stopping to wait for her to catch up. She always referred to this family experience as being one of the most fulfilling in her life. So it was not surprising that she was visiting this village, and then the scene shifted to her riding a bike again in a wooded area in some other beyond life dimension with the grandfather, who was called Opa.

Each time I saw Diana in these motion pictures, I felt a profound range of feelings. I was mesmerized, sometimes feeling as if in a dream. Other times I became so engrossed in how real she seemed as she visited different places in the earth realm that I would think momentarily, *how could I be seeing her, she died?* Then I would quickly challenge myself, *she didn't die, she transitioned, she passed.* Most of the time I was just happy seeing her as she is now. Happy is too limiting a word to describe what I was feeling. But then I felt more determined than ever to actually enter into the dimensions where she was now existing to see her, to connect with her.

So today as I was lying on my mat, I heard the voice of Wily Wizard in my consciousness say, "You are ready. Now you need to look at your list, and visualize where Diana might want to be, whom she might want to visit, and as you focus, you should be able to journey into a specific beyond life dimension. Don't just focus on Diana at this stage. But I caution you to remain patient. Focus more on the experience of journeying than on what you are trying to achieve… Don't just focus on Diana but who and where she might want to be." I lay there feeling excited with the hope of being able to actually find her and enjoy her presence again.

Wily Wizard said I had reached the phase of journeying that I had been trying so long to achieve. I would get a good sleep tonight, and then I would look at that list I made and hope to begin my journeying to actual beyond life dimensions. Did he say something about not focusing so much on what I am trying to achieve, and not just on Diana? I don't know if I can do that, but at least I vowed to try to be patient.

My First Attempt to Journey Into Beyond Life Dimensions

As I lay down on my mat, I felt a strong sense of anticipation. This would be my first journey, or at least my first attempt to journey into beyond life dimensions. I knew Wily Wizard told me to focus on someone or someplace Diana might be inclined to visit or be, but in my excitement I could only envision Diana. I wanted to find her so much, to reconnect with her. I had been seeing her for these past weeks in these so-called motion pictures that I guess Wily Wizard had been allowing me to see, but now he said I would be able to actually journey into these dimensions. And I knew I was conveniently not acknowledging the apparent difficulties I might face actually connecting with her. I am an eternal optimist—I hoped that concept "eternal" would be of some help to me, even though I knew I was taking it out of context. I then realized I was just playing word games in my mind—being a bit nervous...

So I began to breathe rhythmically and tried to still my mind. I focused my attention on the music of Omar Akram's album, *Echoes of Love.* The image of Diana kept drifting into my consciousness, but I continued to focus my attention on my breathing, the music, and opening my consciousness to journeying into beyond life dimensions.

Suddenly I found myself in the middle of what looked like a sea of pulsating, undulating energy, like what I had been seeing when I was floating in what seemed like wa-ter, and later what I had seen at times when I was watch-ing Diana in her different activities and forms. This was different, though—I seemed to be standing in the mid-dle of essences of being blended together to form one large mass of energy. I could distinguish different colors and shapes, just as a sea of water would reflect differ-ent colors, depending on changes in light and weather. These different colors and shapes seemed to be ema-nating from within the different essences of being that were joined—blended—together. I wondered if one of them was Diana, but how could I tell? I was standing on what appeared to be a small island—surrounded by this sea of essences that seemed to extend forever in all directions.

Then I heard a voice say, "You did not take my advice." I realized Wily Wizard was now standing beside me.

"What do you mean?" I said defensively, even though I knew what he meant.

"Yes, you do know what I mean," Wily Wizard said stern-ly, but then softened his tone. "It is understandable that you will make a few mistakes during these early phases of journeying, but you have to try and take my guidance. I asked you to specifically focus on someone or some-place Diana might want to visit or create within her consciousness in beyond life dimensions, but I see you chose to just think of Diana when you began."

"Yes, you're right," I admitted. "I couldn't get her image

out of my mind. I was only able to focus my spiritual imagination on the image of Diana. I did make that list, and I will use it the next time I try to journey. But is Diana somewhere here?"

"You are looking at something like a sea of essences of beings, as your consciousness has conceptualized. To use your concept, this is a sea of interconnected essences of being—as they often exist together in these beyond life dimensions. What you have to remember is that each of the separate essences of consciousness exists in multiple dimensions—each is in different places than what you are now visualizing here, while at the same time they are always blended and connected with each other."

"That's incredible, but then do they know what every other consciousness is thinking or experiencing?"

"Hmm, I'll try to answer, but after that I want you to get back to your own body consciousness in your realm so you can prepare for the next journey—this time in the right way."

"Yes, ok. I will do that," I said a bit sheepishly.

"So just as I told you. Essences of being in beyond life dimensions can't know everything about what's going on with every other essence of being, even if they are always interconnected on some levels. We do not possess an infinite awareness. But we are able to be aware of the fullness of being of those essences that we are closely interacting with for whatever purpose. There is a lot more to this, but now I want to help you get back to your own body consciousness. By the way, after you experience a few successes of making a journey in the way I have told you to, it will be ok if you only want to focus on the image of Diana from time to time—but wait until you have a few successful journeys."

I nodded, and then I took one more look at the beauty of the sea of essences I was standing in the midst of. Even though I had not done this right in my first attempt, I felt a deep sense of appreciation and awe for being so close to somewhere Diana might also be, and so close to… an infinite sea of spiritual essences.

Then I found myself awake on my mat with the music from *Echoes of Love* still playing.

Connecting with George Harrison

Before I lay down on my mat to try to reenter the beyond life realms, I looked at my list of people who had also passed with whom Diana might want to connect and visit. I decided I'd try to focus on George Harrison. So I asked Alexa to play and repeat "My Sweet Lord."

I don't know how many times Diana and I listened to "My Sweet Lord" during the past five years. We both were so familiar and comfortable with this song. We probably listened to it at least once each day. I enjoyed listening to her singing with George Harrison up until she stopped singing within the last month before she passed. She never forgot the lyrics of songs she loved, even as her Alzheimer's progressed, even though she forgot almost everything else—even who George Harrison was.

I lay down and started my breathing ritual, clearing my mind of anything other than finding George Harrison, hoping Diana might be visiting him. I let my inner self merge with the repetitive rhythms of the phrase, "My Sweet Lord, I really want to see you, really want to be with you…"

Suddenly I found myself walking in a garden similar to where I had first seen Wily Wizard. I wondered if all specific beyond life dimensions were gardens. This garden was not wild, but not unnaturally manicured, either. As before, I saw a variety of energy forms, which must be essences of unique spiritual beings, floating in the air throughout the garden, changing shapes and colors with various shades and intensities of what reminded me of a rainbow spectrum. They were stunning, and if I had not been so intent on finding George Harrison and Diana, I could imagine spending my time in this dimension just watching these various transforming essences of beauty—maybe somehow blending with them. As I continued my walk thought the garden, I also noticed peacocks with their iridescent tail feathers spread wide, red-purple flamingos and blue jays flying from limb to limb of various trees. I saw a pleasant blend of bushes and flowers. I particularly noticed large areas of vibrant orange tulips that seemed to add to my sense of well-being and excitement for finally arriving in a specific dimension.

As I walked through the garden, the sounds of eastern music began to surround me, with rhythms of the sitar and tabla along with the soothing sounds of a flute. The song was familiar, but I could not remember where I had heard it.

Then I heard someone say, "You are listening to 'Inner Light,' one of the first songs I wrote after being exposed to northern Indian Hindustan classical music. This song is based upon part of Lao-Tzu's poem in which the last stanza begins with the line, 'Arrive without traveling'..."

I still could not see anyone, but I saw an essence shaped in the form of a white and lilac colored lotus. Suddenly it transformed into a human that looked like George Harrison, wearing cream-colored shirt and pants. He had long black hair, as he did when he had embraced the eastern music from his connections with Ravi Shankar, who had become one of his spiritual and musical teachers while both were living in the earth realm.

"Sorry about not greeting you in my earth realm human form sooner," George Harrison said as I came closer to him. "I sometimes forget the form I'm in—well, most often I'm not in a constant form, but what I mean is, I should have been more thoughtful about the form that would be best to greet you."

"You are George Harrison, right?" I asked.

"Yes, I am the essence that was George Harrison in my most recent life in a physical form... in the earth realm. Anyway, let me welcome you." He put his hands together in front of his face and bowed his head. He was now sitting on a bench, similar to the one that Wily Wizard was sitting on when I met him. The music, the freshness of the greenery mixed with the array of flowers and swirling essences gave me a peaceful feeling.

"Do you mind if I sit on this bench across from you?" I asked.

"Please do sit. I was expecting you."

"How...?" I started to ask.

He looked at me with his intense but engaging eyes. He smiled, "You are well-known in these dimensions—at least by some... some who may be important for you to meet if you continue your journeys, if you continue your quest."

"Then you know that I'm trying to find my love partner, Diana, who passed away. And you must know I am intending on continuing my journeys until I fulfill my promise to connect with her. Can you tell me if you have seen her?"

He did not answer me right way, but it seemed his expression softened. "Yes, I have seen her," he finally said.

I was about to ask if Diana was still close by, but he responded, "No, she went on her way. But what a lovely essence of being she is!"

"You read my mind?'

"Of course, we don't really need to talk in these dimensions, but since you are a visitor—a type of essence we don't see here that much—we try to accommodate."

Instead of talking I thought, *How is she doing? Can you tell me anything about her?*

"Oh, she's doing quite well," George Harrison said out loud. "You know, when I got here, when I passed, I felt so at ease, sublime even. I had prepared for my passing and was fortunate to have the type of spiritual guidance I was exposed to during my earth life. I had developed an attunement to these spiritual dimensions. I had to work at it while living in the earth realm, but eventually it came more naturally to me, and I was so happy when I found myself existing here. After I transitioned here, I realized it was so much like what I had come to believe from studying with my earth-based teachers. I felt fulfilled. My period of adjustment here was very short."

He paused again, and he seemed in a pleasant reverie. After a few minutes, he continued.

"But your Diana, I could tell that she was already mostly adjusted and attuned to this reality, as if she had been here long before she actually transitioned. She seems to be enjoying so much getting in touch and interacting with all the other sides of herself. She is quite special. And she has a voice like a pearl that seems to emanate from her nurturing soul, a soul that I feel must have been able to consistently smooth out rough edges as she lived her life in the earth realm."

 "You heard her sing?"

"Yes, she wanted me to sing 'My Sweet Lord' with her, which was very pleasant, but what really surprised me was that she wanted me to then sing 'Wah Wah' with her. That surprised me."

I smiled. "She really liked singing 'Wah Wah,' too. She sang it a lot."

"She seemed to know that 'Wah Wah' was one my first spiritual songs I felt confident bringing to John, Paul, and Ringo while we were still together as the Beatles. I appreciated she was aware of that. She also wanted me to sing a number of my other spiritual songs, such as 'Inner Light'..."

My attention focused again on the music I first heard when walking through this garden. I realized I had been so focused on meeting George Harrison that the music faded into the background of my consciousness.

"No, I softened the music and pulled it into the background of your consciousness so we could visit without too much distraction."

I had so many questions for him. But he continued, "I promise, all your questions will eventually be answered. But I want to tell you why I created this song for you to hear. I thought about this song when I became aware that you would attempt to journey into beyond earth life dimensions to find Diana. This song's lyrics should have a special meaning for you."

And then he sang the following lyrics, accompanied by the eastern music that he had written:

"Without going out my door
I can know all things on Earth
Without looking out my window
I could know the ways of Heaven…
Arrive without travelling…"

George Harrison stopped singing and said, "You are and will be traveling on amazing journeys to many different dimensions—without leaving your home, without looking consciously out the physical window of your home, but by opening your perceptions to your spiritual imagination, to beyond life dimensions. All life forms on earth have this capacity, but few try to develop it. Few journey into the inner world, into beyond life dimensions, as you are doing. You've already arrived without physically traveling. I'm happy for you."

"I'm also happy I can do this. It seems like I've arrived somewhere in some beyond life dimension, but I haven't yet arrived where Diana is."

"First let me emphasize again that Diana is well in her existence in these dimensions. She seems to know her way around. When she came to me, she wanted to tell me how much my music meant to her, and also she asked me to teach her to play the guitar in the ways I did, combining not just Northern India but also other genres of western music."

I smiled, thinking of when I first met Diana. She had expressed that she really wanted to learn to play the electric guitar, and I bought one for her birthday shortly after we had started living together. She tried to learn for a while, but never seemed to get the hang of it, and eventually she gave it to someone else in the family. But even though she did not learn to play a musical instrument, her sensitivities for both passionate and spiritual music always seemed quite developed.

"Before she came to me she visited with Ravi Shankar. That impressed me quite a lot." George Harrison chuckled. "She got him to teach her to play the Sitar. "

"How could she learn that so quickly?" I wondered.

"Leaning skills in these dimensions is just a matter of imagining you know how to do what you want to do. We can create music within our essence with what you refer to as the spiritual consciousness of our being."

"But why did she have to ask you and Ravi Shankar to teach her?" I asked.

"We develop and integrate and express all the different sides of our being not just by using our spiritual imagination, but also by interacting with other essences of being. At times we can revert to what appear to be physical forms that we used to exist within or some other physical form in order to allow us to more fully develop, integrate, and express a more complete spiritual state of soul being.

"I sort of understand, but would you explain a little more about what you mean by spiritual state of soul being?"

"Wily Wizard would be the one who should be explaining all this to you, but I'll explain what I can," George Harrison said. "All essences of being throughout each of our existences in different forms and in different dimensions—especially in beyond physical life dimensions—have a common process of development to evolve through. First, as I have explained, each essence of being is meant to develop and then integrate different parts or sides of being into its unique consciousness –into the wholeness of its spiritual being. But that's only the first part of the process of achieving a state of spiritual being. The ultimate purpose is not just to achieve a more complete holistic state of being, but then to use the ways of being, skills, and understandings to contribute to the well-being of others as well as to all beyond life dimensions and physical realms."

He continued, "Each essence of being through its process of existing continues to develop its uniqueness by how it chooses to use the common sides of being—what some people in your earth realm call archetypes. There is a polarity that exists—that has always existed between uniqueness of being and the commonality that connects all essences of being. Blending these polarities of uniqueness and commonality leads to more evolved states of being."

Many questions came to my mind. I asked, "Some religions in our earth realm say that the goal of spiritual evolvement is to achieve a state of being where one dissolves back into the spiritual unity rather than having to continue to exist in a unique state of consciousness. Is that wrong?"

George Harrison thought for a moment, and then said, "Every essence of being in every realm and dimension already exists within what you refer to as spiritual unity. The process of development involves recognizing what already exists as an actuality, and then developing and expressing the qualities that we choose to express within the uniqueness of our beings. In Diana's case, she is learning the skills of playing the different types of musical instruments for the spiritual joy of immersing herself more fully in the music expressions. But she is also expanding her ways of assisting others to experience the higher octaves of being in spiritual dimensions. Your love partner has a unique gift of creating beauty and exotic pleasures in a variety of ways, including singing, playing a musical instrument, dancing, painting— and probably in many other ways—just as she did in the earth realm."

 "So in the earth realm, an individual has to work at developing skills and techniques and mental understandings. Whereas in these beyond life dimensions, all of that comes naturally, but it is just a matter of focusing on what an essence of being wants to develop and use at any given time. I have so many more questions. I want to learn as much as I can."

"You will be able to understand more as you continue on your journeys and you spend more time with Wily Wizard," George Harrison responded.

I suddenly realized I might not be able to stay in this dimension, in my state of journeying into the beyond physical life dimension very much longer. I asked George Harrison again if he knew where Diana intended to go next.

"No, not specifically, but I think she said she wanted to find John Lennon." George shook his head but smiled. "I can understand that—But I don't know where John is half the time, even though we have remained quite connected. He is even more of an explorer than I am, while quite less than Diana is. She is so intent on integrating and expressing all the different sides of herself."

"Can you tell me other people she might be seeing?"

"She mentioned some of her family who had passed, and a few other musicians. Oh, she wanted to find Pavarotti. And then she said she wanted to recreate and visit some of her favorite earth places. I think she mentioned Prague, Bavaria and Paris."

All that makes sense, I thought. With what George Harrison was saying, it seemed Diana was so familiar and adept with being in these dimensions. I always felt she was an old soul, and maybe she has existed here often in between a number of past lives and has reincarnated a number of times... maybe she doesn't have to any longer?

George sighed and said, "I don't know the answer to that. Maybe Wily Wizard might know and might be willing to tell you if he does know. You never know what to expect from Wily Wizard."

I stood up to leave. "I guess I should be returning, so I can prepare for my next journey."

George said in a tone of voice as if he were offended, "Hey, but you haven't asked me to sing another one of my songs."

"Oh, I'm so sorry. I didn't want to impose."

"I'm just kidding with you," he said. "It's actually quite nice to have someone talk with me for a reason other than hearing me create my singing or guitar playing. Even though your main purpose for connecting with me was because you wanted to find your lovely companion.

But that's fine. While living on earth I always felt romantic, intimate love was one of the ways the essence of spirituality—transcending the self—could be experienced."

"I believe that also, and I really am excited that I was able to find and visit with you—well, your essence of being—about all this. Thank you!"

As I was preparing to leave, I stopped for a moment to take in the beauty of this garden one more time. I looked around at the variety of red, violet, yellow flowers and the deep rich green of the plants, the swirling essences, some floating through what seemed to be blue sky, others existing as if they were statues of some sort.

I turned back to George Harrison and asked, "Do all the dimensions in the beyond or after life always look like gardens?"

"No, but it's convenient and pleasant for the few travelers like you. If you continue your journeys, I assume you will visit a variety of other dimensions that either you or whomever you will be visiting will be envisioning."

I stood looking at George for a moment, and finally got up the courage to ask him to sing, "My Sweet Lord."

He smiled. "I'll start, but you will awake soon to Alexa still playing my song."

It seemed a bit strange that he mentioned Alexa, but I am learning that essences of being in this dimension seem to be able to know the thoughts and expressions and activities of those they are interacting with. He started singing, and I felt not only feelings of love, but also as though Diana were singing to me, surrounding me with her words.

Then I work up, and yes, Alexa had continued to repeat "My Sweet Lord." I lay on my mat for a while listening to "My Sweet Lord," thinking of my visit with George Harrison and feeling hopeful I would find Diana soon. After all, she had just been with George Harrison.

I might try to find John Lennon next. Or maybe I might imagine visiting places like Prague or Paris. I felt I was so close to connecting with my cosmic companion.

A Place Like Prague

Earlier this evening I lay down on my mat and began the ritual I hoped would allow me to enter into the beyond life dimensions. I decided to put all my intent and concentration of feelings on reaching a place like Prague. All day I'd been thinking of the many times Diana and I had visited this city's old town area, which we felt made Prague the most beautiful, dramatic, spiritual, magical, and mysterious city of Europe. I had a strong feeling that Diana would want to visit a place like Prague—if such existed in some other dimension. I started to debate how could there be such a place, how could I find it in multiple dimensions, but I stopped this line of thinking.

I took a deep breath, and envisioned Diana walking along a narrow, curved, ancient street like ones we had walked when we often visited Prague together—I was listening to Omar Akram's mystical album *Secret Journey.* I focused on my strong yearning to connect with Diana again.

When I entered a beyond life dimension, I did find myself walking along a narrow, curved cobblestoned street, as I had envisioned. I was walking alone. I looked around and wondered why I couldn't reach the place where Diana is, especially if I could so easily enter into this place that seemed like Prague? This place did have the look and feel of Prague. On each building I walked by were the types of art forms and expressions I was familiar seeing in the old town Prague in the earth realm—statues of mythological beings, kings and queens, gods and goddesses built above and within entryways, amazing ornately carved wooden windows and doorways, sparkling with jewels embedded in their wooden frames... Yes! This was just like Prague. Maybe Diana would be here. Surely she would create and visit a place like this in the essence of her consciousness.

As I walked through an open old town square, I could see a multitude of large cathedrals and buildings with spires, towers, and domes and large vertical windows– all perhaps meant to bring my awareness upward to connect with even more expansive dimensions. Then, as I walked from the square into an alleyway under curved arches, I felt as if I were moving through a portal into another part of this deeply mysterious inner dimension.

As I continued to walk through the narrow, curved streets and alleyways, I looked at the frescos painted on cream and beige stucco buildings. All of the art and buildings reminded me of the amazing mixture of Romanesque, Gothic, Art Nouveau, Baroque, and more modern architectural styles that remained unscathed through the centuries in the Prague of the earth realm, seemingly protected by magical or spiritual overseers from wars or other means of senseless destruction.

In the earth realm Prague's frescos depicted its historical kings and queens but also the proletariat, honoring the working class during the Soviet Union's occupation of Prague in the earth realm. But in this dimension, I was seeing statues and frescos that were the types of swirling essences I had seen in the gardens I had visited first with Wily Wizard and then with George Harrison—but these swirling art essences were forming into scenes of strange landscapes, strange beings, strange shapes and blends of colors, as if they were some kind of imaginative streaming videos.

I began to notice that the imagery also displayed witty and humorous scenes and colorful street art. I was reminded of the John Lennon wall where Diana and I had visited, where people could paint and scribble their thoughts and remembrances, and I decided I would perhaps try to find John Lennon in one of my next journeys.

I kept exploring, walking down cobblestone streets and alleys, under archways. I wanted Diana to be here so much. I felt her presence. While walking along one of the alleyways, I noticed what looked like four different swirling, glowing essences of colors above me, lining the edge of a red tile roof on a three-story light brown stucco building with many tall dark wood windows—these essences were not just glowing, but pulsating with a vibrant energy. I stopped and stood gazing, mesmerized by these four swirling energy essences.

Suddenly, one by one, these globes separated from their places on the building and floated gracefully down to the street in front of me. They were flowing together in a harmonious way that lifted my spirits. I felt I was watching a most exquisite light show.

As these lovely essences floated in front of me, they seemed to be emoting intense feelings of peace and happiness. I felt they were flowing within my consciousness, giving me gifts of connection, encouragement, and hope. I began to cry—as Diana often said—with tears of joy. I stood there smiling and crying.

Then, each of these essences floated down closer to the cobblestones, and as they did, they changed into human forms—one was a young man, one an older man, the next a young woman, and the last an older woman. They were dressed in simple, casual clothes, cream-colored pants and tops. Each wore dark leather sandals.

They move closer and hovered near me in a half-circle. I felt deep feelings of being nurtured, as if they were cuddling me within their presences.

"You are searching for someone you love who recently passed," the older man said. "I can see the image of her—of a woman named Diana, emanating from your essence."

 "We talked with her not long ago," the young woman said.

"How long ago?" I asked excitedly, hoping she would still be in this Prague-like realm.

"Time is not something we can address, but she…" then she stopped as she looked at the older woman.

The young woman looked back at me, her expression seeming even more soothing, and said, "It's a magical thing when someone like you, who has not fully passed from your physical form, can enter these dimensions beyond your life, and even more to try to find someone you love who has passed. Very romantic, spiritually romantic."

I sensed they were avoiding answering my question about Diana. I thought I'd try to find out more about them before I asked them again. I felt so good in their presence.

"Is this where your home is? Do you always exist here as glowing essences on this building?"

"Actually no," the old man responded. "We're just resting before each of us continues our own separate journeys—and we like to provide other essences of beings who drift by pleasurable performances and interactions. We often change into different forms depending on who we are connecting with."

"But we don't often meet someone like you who still exists in a realm like your earth. This is so exciting!" The younger man said.

"Quite impressive," the older man said.

"I am amazed myself and thankful for being able to experience these other dimensions. It has relieved my fear of dying."

"You have nothing to fear," the younger woman responded. "Nobody does, but it is natural that people who haven't experienced these dimensions might be fearful—especially with many of the fearful religious beliefs that have been formulated and perpetuated on your earth realm by those who seem to want to control others...."

"How did you come together?"

"We just naturally flowed together...," the young woman said.

"Were all of you alive on earth?" I asked

"No, but we all have existed in different physical realms, similar to those on earth," the young man said. "We have all lived in realms where we had to exist in some type of physical and time-based forms, like the human body we are projecting to you now. It is true that the physical forms can allow for a nice range of physical pleasures to be experienced, but when essences exist in physical forms it is so difficult to develop and remain open to spiritual, psychic, and imaginative capacities."

The younger woman then said, "But you are here now—you've accomplished the ability to journey into these dimensions. I wonder if you could shift your essence into the types of form you first saw us in—your body is not here—the essence of your being is here."

"I don't know how to do what you are suggesting—to shift into a flowing essence of being like you were when I first saw you."

"You might be able to learn to change shapes like we essences of being can," the old man said. "Perhaps if you keep journeying to these dimensions, but to use your frame of reference, it might take time. That's a conundrum, by the way. You are still perceiving the experiences you are having in a time-space frame of reference, yet in these dimensions there is no time—but since you are not actually existing in beyond life dimensions, you are still limited a bit by the time it takes for you to develop abilities that exist naturally for us when we fully reach and will remain in these afterlife multi-dimensions."

I thought about what he was saying, and it did seem to be a conundrum, but I thought I understood what he way meaning. "Can I ask you another question?"

"That's fine with us—most of us, " the younger woman said, looking the old woman.

"Well, ok," I said. "How come you are taking on different human forms? And are you each different genders and ages?" I really wanted to ask them about Diana again, but I was also curious about the nature of these essences of being.

"No, no," the older man laughed. "In beyond life dimensions essences contain all the diverse ways of being that exist in unbalanced patterns in physical realms. We're just choosing forms that would allow you to be at ease talking with us."

At this point I decided to try again to see if they could help me find Diana. Most of them, except the older woman who had not talked, seemed quite willing to communicate with me.

'You said you have seen Diana. Is she somewhere here in this place like Prague? I feel she is so close."

They didn't respond right away. They were looking at the older woman who had remaining silent. Finally the young man spoke, "As we said, we have seen her, but we are sure…"

The younger man stopped talking and looked at the old woman, who had not spoken, at least in a way I could hear. But something was going on.

I turned to the older woman and asked, "What are you not telling me? Please tell me if you know if I could find her."

The older woman finally spoke. Her voice seemed to caress and sooth me, even as I did not like what she was saying. "The woman you are seeking—your love partner when you were on earth—is truly comfortable in this dimension and has been doing things she needs and wants to do to continue on her multi-dimensional spirals of growth. She asked me—us—to give you her deep love, and that she will try to connect with you when she can." And then the older woman became more serious, "I do have to warn you, though, that you may not be able to find Diana as you want her to be. But you will be enhanced through these experiences—just know that— these journeys will allow you to continue to blossom and evolve." And then she turned back into her glowing form and floated back up to her place on the building.

The older man and younger man also turned back into their glowing forms and floated back up.

"But I want to find her…" I said as they floated away.

The younger woman came close to me, and in a lower, whispering voice said, "I believe you will find her. We know nothing of the future in our existences in these dimensions—there are so many possible futures—but anyway, please don't give up. I believe Diana doesn't want you to give up." And she changed her form and floated back up to her place on the building.

I stood for a while gazing up at the glowing, swirling essences, feeling such a mixture of my own swirling feelings. Being in the presence of these essences of being had been pleasant, but then what the older woman said made me feel discouraged. And yet the younger woman had offered me the encouragement that I so needed.

I felt like continuing my search in this place like Prague, but then I woke up on the mat in the meditation room. I took a deep breath and tried to center my emotions. After a few moments of lying in silence, reminiscing of the many times Diana and I walked together throughout the exquisite and mysterious streets of Prague, I resolved to continue my journeys to fulfill my promise and desire to reconnect with Diana. I realized, though, that I needed to allow my consciousness some time to regenerate—at least a day or two—before I could re-enter another beyond life dimension, but I was determined to continue.

Entering the Forest—Golden Butterflies and the Tantric Snake

When I next prepared to journey into the beyond life dimensions, I decided I would just focus on Diana herself again, and not a person or place she might be visiting. Wily Wizard said I could continue to try different types of intentional envisioning from time to time to see if my abilities have developed enough to allow me to journey into a specific dimension where Diana might be.

Before I had lain down on my mat I had been listening to some of our favorite songs by Pink Martini. The song playing was "The Butterfly Song." I heard the lyrics, "If you love a butterfly let it be." I have always liked the meaning of this song, but it wasn't what I wanted to focus on as I was preparing for my next journey. So I asked Alexa to play Omar Akram's instrumental music, which I felt would be more conducive to allowing my consciousness to become open to entering into beyond life dimensions.

When I entered a beyond life dimension this time, I was startled to see Diana in the far distance near the edge of a forest. She was quite far away, but I still could see, though barely, that she was in her physical earth form.

She was walking amongst a large patch of golden yellow sunflowers. I saw her bend down and cup some of these wildflowers in her hands. I watched her raise her arms up above her head and release the petals she was holding. These flowers changed into golden butterflies that flew into the sky and scattered into the forest. She reached down to gather petals two or three more times, each time releasing the petals to become golden butterflies that spread out in stunningly beautiful patterns in the sky and then disappeared into the forest.

I had already started running across the field, calling her name. She didn't look my way, and suddenly she turned and entered the forest. The distance to the edge of the forest was farther than I expected, but finally I reached the place where she had entered the forest, and I saw there was a path. I hurried into the forest on the path.

As I entered the forest I strongly sensed her presence and felt she could not have gone far. As I walked down the path into the forest, I could hear harmonious singing of birds in the trees above me. Some of the golden butterflies flew around me. I loudly called Diana's name over and over again but heard no response.

Then, to my dismay, I came to a place in the forest where the path forked in two directions. Which way did she go? I knelt down, but I could not see any imprints she might have made in the dirt path—then I shook my head, realizing she would probably not be making any footprints, anyway. Was she real? Did the body in which she appeared have physical substance and weight? Probably not. There was so much I did not understand.

If I had a chance of catching up to her, I had to quickly decide which path to take. I noticed that many of the butterflies were flying in the direction of the left pathway, so I decided to follow them. As I walked deeper into the forest, it became denser and denser. What had been park-like was becoming wilder and more jungle-like, with thickening growths of brambles and what looked like dark grass spreading out into the forest in both directions from the path. The trees were closer together, with more vines twisting and spreading across their lower limbs. I had to duck under some of the vines as I kept walking.

I could see and hear what seemed like thrushes singing and perching on higher limbs, and I began to see colorful yellow and blue feathered macaws perched on the lower limbs and what looked like monkeys swinging on vines. I heard strange animal sounds—were they tigers or cougars or some other kind of dangerous species? I was beginning to feel a little nervous about going deeper into this wild forest, but I still felt the presence of Diana—maybe I was fooling myself, hoping I would catch up to her, but I decided I had to keep going.

The path was becoming narrower, and the thickening undergrowth and vines were slowing my progress. Suddenly, as I turned a corner of the path, I came face to face with a large python-like black snake hanging from a lower branch of a tree. Its head was inches away from my face, and I could see into its blue-gray eyes with their vivid dark purple centers. Looking deeply into its eyes, which seemed like portals to another vast mysterious dimension, I instantly became immobile as though I were being hypnotized. But then I felt an unexpected feeling of passion, as if this snake was something I was meant to embrace.

I could not move. I was completely at the mercy of what this snake wanted to do to me. I thought I remembered that pythons were not poisonous, but was it going to squeeze me, or rather my consciousness, to death? I wasn't thinking clearly or maybe I would have remembered what Wily Wizard had said to me—everything is benevolent in the beyond life realms, but he also told me there were limits to what my earth consciousness could withstand. He said he would try to be there to protect me when it mattered.

Did it matter now? I wondered as I looked into the eyes of this huge shake. But somehow I felt it didn't matter. I could not move anyway. I was completely under the spell of this snake as I continued to feel a tingling of excitement throughout my body.

The snake began to move toward me, but I felt no fear, and strangely even more excitement. I watched as the snake dipped down toward my feet and began to curl itself around my legs, sliding upward as it continued to curve itself around my thighs, pelvic area, chest, and then around my neck, and finally the head of the snake came back around to face me. I began to feel a sensual feeling of pleasure throughout my body and what felt like some kind of tantric-like orgasmic experience. The snake then nestled its head against my cheek, and I felt a warmth, a sense of caring mixed with the passion I was also feeling....

And then I woke up on the mat in the meditation room. I was not able to move. My body, which of course had not accompanied me on this journey, felt so alive, and I just lay there enjoying the fullness of pleasure and emotional release I had experienced with that snake curled around me. Could that snake be Diana—if so, why wouldn't she have shown herself to me as she had appeared at the edge of the forest? Maybe imagining that the snake was Diana was just a desperate fantasy of mine, wanting to reconnect with her no matter in what form or way it might occur.

I knew I would have to try to journey back to this forest and take the other path to see if I could find Diana. I decided I would not wait. I knew that I usually needed a few days rest before I could re-enter the beyond life realms, but I felt so alive. I wanted to take the other path right away. At least, I had seen Diana in a dimension I was also in... for the first time since she passed.

But I have to admit, for just a second I felt tempted by what I experienced with this snake to take the left path again. In a spiritual sense, I knew that snakes symbolize the potential for the raising of passions and psychic energies to exquisite, transforming levels. I felt I experienced some of that, but however good it felt, I knew if I could get back to this forest, I would take the other fork of the path next time, and maybe this path would lead me to Diana in the form of how she was on the earth realm, in a form of being that would allow me to communicate and interact more fully with her.

The Wild River

I closed my eyes while I listened to the music of Omar Akram's album *Free As A Bird,* and I imagined myself standing on the path where it had forked into two directions in the forest where I had just journeyed. I took rhythmic, steady breaths—letting the music and the image of Diana in the forest flow through my consciousness.

At some point I did find myself standing on the path I had envisioned, where it forked into two directions. This time I took the other path and hurried deeper into the forest. As before, the forest became denser and denser, but I kept going.

After a while, I came out of the forest and was standing at the edge of a wide river. Forests were on each side of the river, and there were banks of small rocks and boulders between the forests and the river. I sat on a large rock and contemplated what I should do. I brought the image of Diana to my mind again.

Why would I end up by this wide, wild river... unless Diana was somewhere around? I called Diana's name— at least in my mind. It seems everyone who is nearby hears everything in these dimensions anyway. So maybe she could hear me, now that I was here.

I saw a movement on the other side of the river at the forest edge down a way from where I was sitting. I jumped up and made my way down to where I saw something on the other bank. I was able to see that a woman who looked like Diana had emerged from the forest, and she was with a young boy—from the distance it looked like it could be Henry, my grandson, who recently passed away suddenly and sadly at the age of fourteen from a heart attack.

I tried to call out to them, but the sounds of the river rapids were too loud. Surely they could hear me, or at least notice me. *Why couldn't I just float across?* I wondered, *Isn't that what these essences in these realms are capable of doing?* The beings I met in Prague thought I could do that, if not then, maybe eventually.

I could still see that this woman, who could be Diana—her hair and stature looked like Diana—stood with the boy who could be Henry. I waved to try to get their attention, but the two of them seemed to be focusing so intently on each other. They both were wearing shorts and t-shirts.

Then, to my surprise, she and Henry each pulled what looked like surfboards from the forest's edge. They were laughing and so engaged with each other.

I was confused a bit, because Diana had been a little afraid of swimming in rivers or the sea when she was alive. She had almost drowned when she was a child, but I also felt her fear had more to do with her Pisces sun sign—transpersonal water—surrounded by mostly earth signs in her psyche. When she was alive, she needed to remain firmly in the earth realm, and that allowed her to imbue the earthy environments she created and lived with the magic from her spiritually imaginative connections, her perceptions she received consciously and unconsciously from the ethereal, aesthetic, visionary dimensions.

I thought maybe I should just dive into the river and see what happens—surely I could get across somehow, even though the river and rapids looked so wild, and the waters could be deep with frightfully strong currents.

I knelt down and put my hand in the water—it felt freezing, and I could also feel how strong the currents were. How come I couldn't just change the nature of the river with my imagination or even make the river disappear? *I'll have to ask Wily Wizard when I see him again,* I thought.

Next thing I knew Wily Wizard was sitting beside me. He said, "That's because this river was created by your Diana, and this environment is totally under her control."

"So that is Diana on the other side of the river, and Henry? For sure?"

"Yes."

"Why doesn't she notice me—respond to me?"

"I don't know. You'll have to ask her if you catch up with her."

"But I'm so close."

"Well, just try to enjoy what you can."

Then I noticed that Wily Wizard was wearing what

looked like a wet suit. And suddenly he was also wearing scuba diving equipment and flippers. Then he dove into the river and disappeared under the water.

I looked over at Diana and Henry and gasped as I saw them place their surfboards on the surface of the river, lie down on their respective boards, and let the current take them down the river. I saw them reach across the waters and hold each other's hands before the current temporarily separated them. They flowed side by side on their surfboards down the river. Before I lost sight of them I could see both Diana and Henry were standing up on their surfboards, and then I saw Henry had jumped onto Diana's board. Then they too dove into the river.

What!? was the last thing I remember thinking in amazement before I awoke in my room. I lay on my mat with a mixture of feelings again flowing through me. At least I saw her. And I saw Henry. I was happy about that. Even though the river was wide and wild, I was close to her. Next time I see Wily Wizard, I'll have to ask him why he didn't give me his scuba diving equipment so that I could have perhaps reached Diana. Damn him!—Sorry, Wily Wizard, I quickly thought. I just want to connect with Diana so much. Then a thought came into my mind. Why did he even need such equipment anyway? Wasn't Wily Wizard just an essence of being that could have just changed shapes and floated across the river, or walked across the river?

I realized there is so much I don't understand. Maybe

it is just that Wily Wizard likes trying on different out-
fits, or maybe he's a bit eccentric. *If you are listening,
Wily Wizard,* I thought to myself, *please take that as a
compliment.*

But wow, it was so neat to see Diana surfboarding with
Henry! What other sides of Diana will I be seeing and
experiencing?

Visiting a Beyond Life Art Gallery

A few days after returning from the dimensions of the forest and wild river, I lay down on my mat to prepare for my next journey. Just before lying down, I had been looking at some of Diana's art.

So when I entered this next beyond life dimension, I was not surprised to find myself walking through an art gallery, down a wide hall with what looked like framed paintings hanging on the walls. The framed paintings—I guessed they were paintings—because each frame was covered by a shimmering light azure silk cloth with an ornamental burnt sienna border—cloth coverings that Diana might have sewn or created somehow in this dimension.

Then I noticed the scent of wild musk perfume. Wild musk was one of Diana's favorite perfumes which she wore often. The scent was so strong it evoked feelings of hope that perhaps she was somewhere near.

I could not see any doorways leading to adjoining rooms. This art gallery seemed to consist only of the long hallway that extended far into the distance beyond my sight. I decided to continue walking along the hallway, and maybe I would finally find Diana. The scent of musk, perhaps her musk, remained strong.

As I continued down the hallway, I was surrounded by many essences of being, similar to the ones I had seen in other dimensions, and like the ones I had met in a place like Prague. They were floating around, some hovering in front of different frames, some just floating down the hallway in the direction I was going. I wondered if the ones hovering in front of the different frames could see through the silk cloth coverings. I realized that I was the only human form in this art gallery, but none of the essences seemed to be aware of me or try to interact with me, which was fine, because all I wanted to do was find Diana.

But then I noticed that some of the essences of being flowed through the blue silk cloths and into whatever was behind the frames. This obviously made me curious about what was behind these frames, covered with these sensual-looking cloths. I noticed that each cloth was fluttering gently, as if a breeze was moving through the hallway, even though I could not feel a breeze. Something was gently causing the cloths to dance to some rhythm beyond what I could hear or feel. As I looked down the hallway, I became aware that these lovely cloths were shimmering in some kind of coordinated rhythm, and I could almost hear a piano concerto being played.

I came out of my reverie and finally decided I needed to see what was behind these cloths over the frames. I walked over to the nearest frame and pulled back the cloth. What I saw took my breath away. I was not looking at a painting or drawing, or digital screen of some type—I was looking at a couple lying together on a tropical beach near the sea. They were entwined in each other's arms, and I felt their love, their passion so strongly. I felt as though they were actually existing in another dimension, and the frame I was in front of was a portal into that dimension. I had to let the cloth go and step back. I felt as though I was invading their private intimacy.

After a few moments, I knew I had to see what was in another frame. When I pulled the next cloth back, I found myself looking at a night sky full of stars, shining and pulsating intensely, as if I was not looking at them from the earth, my view filtered through the earth's atmosphere. I began to feel that these stars were reaching out to me, wanting me to dissolve into the frame—and I know it sounds crazy, but I felt I was being invited to become one of the stars in the dimension I was viewing. What seemed even crazier to me was that I wanted to. I wanted to dive into the space within this frame and... experience the cosmic intensity of being a companion to these stars. I don't know how I did it, but I let go of the cloth and stepped back, and as soon as I did the feelings I had been experiencing subsided.

I felt as though I should not look behind any more cloths, and I decided to continue on down the hallway to see if I could find Diana. I could still smell the perfumed scent of musk that brought memories of her sensual essence to me.

I walked further down the hallway, but at one point an essence of being with flowing mauve- and rose-colored energy patterns drifted over and bumped into me gently. I felt an electric current of joyful pleasure, and then a sense of anticipation that the completion of my journey to fulfill my promise was close. The essence of being that touched me then floated over to one of the frames and disappeared through the shimmering blue cloth covering.

I felt again the sense that I was being invited into whatever was within this frame. I walked over to it and became aware that the lovely scent of the musk perfume was even stronger than before. Something or someone perhaps was beckoning me! Maybe Diana was in the dimension within this frame. At this point in my journeying I was beginning to trust my intuitions more and more, and I just went with it. I pulled back the cloth, and I instantly became mesmerized...

I was seeing an Italian courtyard with one small round table in the middle of a patio made of rainbow rock gravel and surrounded by vases filled with an array of dark and light green leafed plants topped with vibrant red, gold, and purple flowers. Two ornate empty wooden chairs with soft velvet purple cushions were facing each other across the small round table. The table was covered with a tablecloth similar to the light blue silk with the sienna border that covered the frames. Not too far from the table was a tall alabaster statue of a man and woman in an embrace, the woman resting her head on the man's shoulder.

On the table in front of both chairs were single glasses of red wine. Beside one of the wine glasses was an open sketch book just like the one that Diana took so often with her on our travels. I then noticed that the wine in the glass by the sketch book was less full than the other one. And then I became aware again of the strong scent of musk. Diana must be close by. I turned my attention to the hallway, and looked around, but I didn't see her or the mauve- and rose-colored essence that had touched me...

I looked back at the Italian courtyard within the frame,

and I felt this urge to enter this space, to try to find and join Diana. I had this feeling that perhaps she had been sketching, drinking a glass of Italian wine, waiting for me to come to her, and she had just stepped away for a moment. I felt all I needed to do was allow my consciousness to journey into this live art piece, just as I had journeyed into these beyond life dimensions.

I was about ready to intentionally focus my consciousness on flowing into this art piece when I heard the voice of someone standing beside me say firmly, "Don't do it."

I turned and saw Wily Wizard standing beside me. He was reaching to pull the cloth back across to cover the frame.

"But I feel she is there. I can smell her perfume so strongly. I can see her sketch book and the wine she has been drinking," I desperately pleaded with him.

"Whether or not she is somewhere near that court-yard, if you allow your consciousness to blend within the frame of that alternate dimension, I don't think you would be able to get back here, and then get back to your body in the earth realm. Just too many layers you would have to get back through. You are not able to do that yet. You are not ready."

I felt so resistant to believing what Wily Wizard was telling me. Hadn't I been able to enter into these beyond life dimensions faster than Wily Wizard and others thought possible? I wanted to take the risk. I made a promise to Diana, and I felt a longing need within me to reconnect with her, to be intertwined with Diana again, and I knew she must be right there near the table in the Italian courtyard. All I had to do was flow into that reality. Then I could be sitting with her drinking wine, enjoying her sketches, and planning our next adventures. I decided to just follow my feelings despite Wily Wizard's concerns.

Just as I was beginning to focus my concentration on entering the dimension inside the frame where I knew Diana had to be, I felt a touch on the back of my head... and the next thing I remember was waking up on my mat. I stood up and yelled, "Dammit Wily Wizard, just let me make my choices. Let me try."

Then I heard in my mind, "Choices you make during these journeys do not just affect you. Such choices are not for you alone to make. Your free will choices have to be balanced with the needs of others in these beyond life dimensions, just as in your earth realm. Especially with the needs of those who now exist in what you sometimes refer as the afterlife, like Diana. As you continue your journeys you will understand more. Accept what I am telling you and be patient if you want to keep being able to journey into these dimensions."

I thought with a sense of resignation, *I guess I don't have a choice.*

"You don't, but try to enjoy what you are experiencing, and you may be able to fulfill your promise as you journey more, as you understand more."

"What more do I need to understand?" I lashed out.

Then I heard Wily Wizard say to me, "Take some deep breaths. Let those frustrated feelings be transformed. Appreciate the amazing spiritual abilities you are developing within yourself—and the connections you are making as you are journeying. And then maybe you might want to go have a real glass of red wine made from grapes grown somewhere on your earth realm. This will help you renew your romantic intent before your next journey."

Connecting With John Lennon

Another try to find my love. This time I decided to see if I could find John Lennon. Why not? Maybe next time I'll search for Luciano Pavarotti. I'd try searching for Andrea Bocelli, if he had passed and was in these realms. I quickly thought, *I'm so glad you haven't passed. The earth needs your inspiring voice, as your songs so often gave transcending musical pleasures to Diana.*

Anyway, before lying down on my mat, I had been listening to a recent remix of Beatles music on the album Love. One particular song combined George Harrison's "Within You Without You" with John Lennon's "Tomorrow Never Knows," which reminded me of the strong connection between George Harrison and John Lennon, especially in their own spiritual development despite their different, unique paths.

As I lay down, I asked Alexa to play and repeat John Lennon's "Starting Over." I closed my eyes, breathing deeply and rhythmically...

I found myself in a room sitting in a chair facing John Lennon. He looked just like I imagined he would with his round glasses and brown shoulder-length hair. I wondered if he really needed those round glasses in these beyond life dimensions.

"It seems you are getting good at this, my man," he said. "And no, I don't need these round glasses, and of course, I don't really exist in this body that you remember me existing in while I lived on earth. But you know by now that I am appearing in this form for your sake."

"Yes, I do know that," I said, "And yes, it does seem to be getting easier to enter into these dimensions. Of course, you were prepared that I would be trying to connect with you."

"Yes... Diana told me."

"And you don't know where she is or how to find her, I assume."

"Well, she did say she was going to try to find some female singers who have passed." he said, smiling. "At least, the essence of the female singers they were during their earth life. As you might already know, we are beyond gender—well, let me say that all genders, ethnicities, races, ways of being, inclinations, etc. are a part of us. Of course, that's the way it was on earth, but most individuals have difficulties reaching levels of consciousness that would allow them to recognize and experience what that's like. I think Yoko and I were on the path to perhaps develop some of that awareness—but of course, I was shot, and that sent me into these other beyond life dimensions where, I have to say, I have experienced levels of consciousness and being that I only imagined in my life on earth Actually, being in these dimensions has given me a profound hope for humanity—I believe the essences of being in human form will continue to thrive and evolve and connect in so many beautiful ways even before they transition to these dimensions."

"Those thoughts are what you and Yoko expressed in "Imagine."

"Yes, that song reflects my faith in human life essences. Now that I've transitioned into these beyond physical life dimensions, I know all essences are one. I always understood that each essence has to filter existence through their unique perspectives based on family, ethnicity, religion, nationalistic influences, and their own natural inclinations—but only up to a certain point. On earth, these unique perspectives too often blind people to the lovely universal connections we all have with each other—and that we are all one in our psyches, in our hearts."

"You know that song has given so many people hope that we all can recognize our spiritual connection to others. I have always recognized the difference between religious beliefs and spirituality."

John said, "When I wrote 'Imagine' it seemed that many people with rigid beliefs such as 'My god is the only true god' could not make that distinction between their divisive beliefs and the interconnectedness that is the true spiritual reality."

As I listened to John Lennon talk, I knew I wanted to find Diana and that's what I mainly wanted to focus on. But I have realized that these journeys are providing me life-changing, spiritual opportunities to interact with essences of being that have much to teach me and share with me. And here I am with John Lennon's essence. I knew we would get back to talking about Diana soon enough. I created an image in my consciousness of me taking a deep breath and relaxing. And I knew breathing doesn't exist in these dimensions, but I also knew that I was really still living in my time-space frame of reference. I was aware that my body would continue to breath back in the earth realm... at least, I hoped so.

"Then let's get back to talking about the love of your life," John Lennon said, responding to my thoughts. "Just as you miss your love partner, I miss sharing my life with Yoko in the sensual earth-time reality. That's why I felt ok about allowing you to connect with me."

"Thank you, but I feel so frustrated. Don't get me wrong, I love being in your presence—oh my god, you are a musician and artist I've admired and enjoyed so much since I was young, but I can't seem to find where Diana is. Here I am, able to shift into this realm in my consciousness, and all I am finding is people who have seen her, but she has just moved on. And then, at times I've seen her in the distance, but can't reach her."

"Life can be tough, can't it? You are still mostly existing in your earth life consciousness, and can't yet fully experience all the amazing potentials and connections that these beyond life dimensions offer."

"What does that actually mean? I am beginning to worry that I have to wait for my own passing to connect with Diana again—that I can't do it through journeying while I am still alive. As much as I love Diana and want to reconnect with her, I do want to live out my life fully, and I would never want to end my life early just to be with her."

"No, no, I'm not saying you will have to wait until you pass to reconnect with Diana. I mean, I would never suggest you commit suicide or anything like that," John said with a concerned expression. "I'm just saying these dimensions are difficult to navigate if you are not wholly here. You may be able to find and connect with your love. You must know that I am as much of a romantic as you are. But for many reasons it is very difficult to find and interact directly with someone to whom you have a lasting and strong loving connection and who has passed."

"As much as I miss the love of my life," I said, "I would never choose to commit suicide—unless perhaps, I had some painful illness that I had no chance of getting relief from, or that would make me unable to live a quality life."

"But your wife developed an illness where she could not think coherently or do all the things she had been capable of... and you kept her alive—and cared for her so lovingly."

"Yes—I feel so good about being able to be with her and care for her during her illness," I said.

"And I'm sure you didn't want to let go of her. I'm not implying you were selfishly keeping her alive just because you did not want to let go of her—even though you knew she could never do what she would consider her quality of life activities that represented her essence. I am aware that you did everything you could to help her make a peaceful transition, to encourage her to go when she was ready."

"Diana had lost her cognitive functioning, but she was still able to connect with all her family and friends in her normal, emotional, loving way."

"That's because she was a highly developed soul being," said John, "but many people haven't developed and established such wonderful connections to spiritual beyond life dimensions, and they just feel frustrated and angry that they cannot continue to do the things they could do before, whether physically or rationally. It is important for humans and all other life forms to open themselves to and embrace spiritual dimensions—it makes transitioning and passing from the earth realm more peaceful and with less resistance. Choosing to live and die when faced with terminal illnesses is not easy. The earth realm provides so much physical pleasure, and then there is the connection between humans and other life forms... I get it."

"I suppose there are many people in these dimensions who have ended their lives through some type of suicide."

"Yes, both for terrible reasons and for good reasons, such as you mentioned—when someone is facing a long and painful illness or losing abilities to function with a sustained quality of life. Consciously choosing to transcend is sometimes a way of acknowledging it is the right time to pass."

"I understand that someone might choose assisted suicide as a form of spiritual healing," I answered, "because as I now understand, once an essence leaves the human body, it becomes healed as it enters beyond life dimensions. But it seems it would be so important for individuals to live out their sparks of life in the earth realm as long they have the abilities to become whom they are meant to be, and to interact emotionally with those they love, and to contribute to the whole of the community."

"Yes, it makes sense if the individual is still able to function well enough to be engaged in active and interactive ways that reflect their uniqueness of being."

I sat back, wondering what I should do next. I realized this visit was not getting me closer to Diana.

"You don't know that," John Lennon said. "But I know you will have to be leaving soon. Do you want to hear me sing?

I thought about my experience with George Harrison, and quickly said, "Yes, would you sing 'Jealous Guy' for me?"

"Hmm, that's the song Diana wanted me to sing, and it was so sweet to hear her whistle with me when she got to that part. Will you be whistling also?"

I smiled and told him no, that was one of her special

skills, not mine. I was finally able to relax with the fond memories of all the times Diana would whistle when that part of the song came on, even during the last weeks of her life.

John started singing the song, and by the time he got to the whistling part, I found myself lying on my mat, listening to John Lennon's whistling song being played on Alexa.

I had not expected a discussion about choosing to let a loved one die, or about assisted suicide, but then again, how could I have ever imagined being able to talk with the essence of John Lennon? I'll continue trying to find Diana, and I know I have to remain patient as well as open to expanding my spiritual awareness and knowledge.

Competition or Cooperation?

On my last beyond life journey, I found myself in the arena of a large circular ancient amphitheater which looked like the ones I have been to in Italy and other parts of Europe, where Romans held vicious fights between gladiators, as well as with lions and other wild animals which were then slain—all of this for the pleasure of spectators. Today's Roman amphitheaters are mostly used for tourist attractions, festivals, and opera performances.

As I looked around in this arena, I saw that I was in the middle of a multitude of essences in human form who were fencing with each other—without protective gear on. I could see that the tip of the foil, the fencing blade, would often touch and even puncture the upper body of the opponent, but none of the fencers seemed to be hurt.

Despite what seemed to be an activity that was bloodless and harmless (at least for the essences of being in this dimension), I quickly realized it would be in my best interest to get out of this arena as quickly as I could. I became nervous that inadvertently I would be punctured or sliced—there were so many essences in physical forms, most human, fencing in the arena.

Then I wondered why I would end up in this type of place when I was trying to find Diana. It didn't even seem like a place Diana would ever want to be—amid competing fencers, even though she did go to various amphitheaters in Verona and a few other cities in Italy to see opera performances. And then as I thought about it more, it didn't make sense that this kind of competition would even exist in what Wily Wizard said were totally benevolent dimensions. Were there darker, more vicious aspects to the beyond world realms than I understood?

I looked for an exit that would allow me to leave this arena before I got run through or sliced. I didn't even have a foil, and of course I didn't have skills to defend myself with a foil, anyway. I knew that my body was safely lying on my mat in my room in the earth realm, but I understood from Wily Wizard that my consciousness could not handle certain things that might happen to me in these beyond life dimensions, and my psychological being would be damaged in my earth life if these things happened. Being stabbed or sliced certainly seemed like something that could cause me severe psychological damage.

All of sudden I felt what must have been the tip of a foil blade touch my back. I was about to run, but I heard a woman command, "Don't move. Don't turn around. I know you should not be here, though I know why you arrived here. I can guide you safely out of this arena if you do exactly as I say. Don't resist. Don't run away. These other fencers should know you are not from this dimension and leave you alone, but there is always the possibility of one of them trying to engage you, not realizing you are just a visitor. Or you could just be at the wrong place at the wrong time and get unintentionally harmed. "

"Ok, I'll do exactly as you instruct," I managed to say, though I did wonder why I was feeling a bit of pain from the point of her foil. I thought that in modern fencing foil or epee blades had rubber tips on them, and why was I feeling physical pain anyway in these beyond life dimensions?

The fencing woman who was supposed to be guiding me out of this arena said, "In these dimensions we are not here to win or hurt each other, and we can't be harmed anyway, so there is no need to use rubber tips. As you know, you are not really totally in this dimension. Your spirit imagination is connected to your body in the earth realm, and everything you are envisioning and experiencing is still connected to your body sensations. I need to escort you out of here quickly. Walk toward the red and blue banner hanging over there. Don't stop. As long as the other sword competitors see I have my sword pointed at your back they won't try to challenge me or you. I don't think."

"You don't think? Don't you know?"

"We can't know everything. Nothing is predestined."

Where have I heard that before, I thought as I started walking.

But I also wondered how being stabbed or sliced in this dimension would affect my body in the earth realm. The fencing woman answered what I was thinking, "Such an unfortunate event would damage your consciousness, not your body... at least initially. When you come out of the trance you are now in... well, you might not even come out of the trance. You might become comatose, and if you did come out of the trance you might exhibit schizophrenic or psychotic symptoms. Someone like Wily Wizard might be able to heal you, but it would take a while and would be uncomfortable for you. We should just avoid that happening."

"Yes, I agree. Let's avoid that."

I thought again about Wily Wizard telling me I could not jump into the river when I saw Diana in one of my earlier journeys. I would have probably drowned, or at least my consciousness would have. And Wily Wizard would not let me flow into the frame in the art gallery. I have to accept that there are limits to what my consciousness will be able to handle in these beyond physical life dimensions.

As we walked toward the flag where the exit apparently was, I had to dodge foils being thrust and swung in my direction. I could feel the swish of the blades jutting past my... consciousness.

I finally asked, "Could you at least tell me why I am here? Why would Diana come here to participate in this kind of competition? It just doesn't seem like her."

"She was not interested in competing. Nobody here is. You need to think of the fencing you are seeing here as a form of what you earth people might call Tai Chi—it's all about movement, concentration, and coordination, but there is more to it in how it is approached in these dimensions."

She stopped talking as we had to move carefully around fencers who were concentrated in one area. Then she continued, "In your earth realm two or more people try to win in these types of activities or other games. But instead, think of teams as two sides of a polarity—opposites that can become complementary blends if they were to find ways of cooperating so that both become more than what each of them could be as just one side of a polarity. When winning or total self-gratification are not the goals, the aim becomes for each side of the polarity to assist the other to perform at the highest levels each can—to achieve a complementary balancing and blending with each other. That's how the pure joy of inter-connectedness is achieved."

She remained quiet as we again maneuvered around a concentrated group of fencers. Then she continued, "I realize that this type of cooperative blending does not occur that often in your earth realm. I know it doesn't happen in games or sports. The closest activity in your earth realm that I can compare this type of joyful blending to is what is supposed to happen during lovemaking—two or more individuals focusing on the pleasures and desires of the partner as much as their own pleasures and desires, which could lead to a wonderful blend of emotions and sensuality in which the two or more lovers temporarily become more than they could be separately."

She continued, "Diana came here to experience the type of complementary balance of skills and movement that I am describing."

What this fencer was telling me made sense. I knew that Diana was never into competition or game playing. This was another example of her trying to experience all sides of herself and continue to develop her wholeness.

As we were nearing the edge of the arena two fencers came in front of us and raised their foils. The fencing woman who was trying to escort me out said quickly, "He is not from this dimension. He is visiting from the earth realm and came here by mistake. If he is damaged, it might be permanent. Let me escort him out."

The fencers immediately stepped aside. I moved through the exit into a darkened passageway with the point of the foil still pressed against my back. Finally, the fencing woman pulled it away.

I was about to turn around and face this woman who had helped me. I was planning on saying, "I suppose Diana has already left?" even though I already knew the answer.

The next thing I was aware of was being on my mat, but I still felt for a second the sensation of a point of a foil pricking my back.

A Place like Istanbul

This afternoon before attempting to enter again into a beyond life dimension in search for Diana, I was thinking about an astrological technique referred to as astro-cartography. This technique is used to identify specific areas on earth, specific cities and countries, specific longitudes and latitudes—that would best enable individuals to not only develop different sides of their natural inclinations and personality potentials but also to be able to experience positive expressions of these different sides of self—such as romantic love, intimacy, artistic creativity, financial and career achievement, discipline, assertiveness, transpersonal, and spiritual growth.

In using this technique to analyze Diana's birth chart, I identified that her spiritual center was connected to various areas of the Middle East—Tehran, Istanbul and Morocco. Diana said she resonated so much with this analysis; she said all of her life she felt a strong affinity with Middle Eastern cultures, in terms of music, art, foods—but of course, not with the patriarchal religious and political practices. She said she often wondered if in one of her past lives she had been roaming the deserts, living simply but attempting to make life pleasurable by cooking with earthy spices and surrounding daily life with exotic cloths, perfumes, dancing, and singing.

We had always wanted to go together to visit cities and areas of the Middle East, and finally in 2001 we were able to visit one of our friends, LaHoma, who was living at the time in Istanbul. Our visit to Istanbul was fulfilling in ways that allowed us to experience the art, spiritual, and cultural patterns of the Middle East. Being in Istanbul at the time brought us so much hope so soon after the 911 attacks on the Twin Towers in New York. We had been a little concerned about traveling to Istanbul, wondering what people there would be feeling about the U.S. But we found sincere empathetic expressions of goodwill and condolences and sorrow about what had happened, and we felt deeply gratified and appreciative. We felt the oneness with all humanity.

Being in Istanbul, a city symbolizing the positive blends of Middle Eastern and European cultures, inspired us and gave us hopeful feelings about humanity. Despite the history of conquest, oppression, and fanaticism that exists in all places in the world, we found the people we met in Istanbul caring, world-conscious, and accepting the diversity of religious practices.

After thinking about this during the day, I decided to focus my intent on journeying to a place like Istanbul. As I closed my eyes, I began my deep breathing while listening to the song "Ya Allah—Woman in a Mosque" from the soundtrack to the movie Bab Aziz. I focused on entering into the alternate dimensions in a place like Istanbul. I had a psychic intuition that Diana was visiting there. Wily Wizard had told me I should go with my intuitions of where Diana might be or have been. He said he felt I was now in tune with her presences in the various dimensions she was existing in, and that I should follow my intuitions. It had been working. I seem to be able to enter into a dimension where she is or has been, but I haven't been able yet to actually connect with her as I had promised. I know, *Wily, I have to be patient—in case you are listening to my thoughts, which I am assuming you are.*

I began the process of clearing my mind, and eventually I found myself walking in a beyond life dimension in front of what resembled the Blue Mosque. I stared up at the tall minarets stretching into the sky, and I noticed there were many more than the six that were on the actual Blue Mosque in the earth realm. I could hear a prayer being sung over a loudspeaker throughout the Sultan Ahmed Square. I was alone in this large, exotic square.

I first tried to enter the Blue Mosque, but the doors were locked. I then decided to make my way to the Hagia Sofia, a place Diana and I had frequented a number of times while we were in Istanbul. It was originally built as a basilica for the Greek Orthodox Church 1500 years ago, when Istanbul was known as Constantinople. In 1453, the Islamic Ottoman empire captured the city and renamed it Istanbul. The Hagia Sofia then became a mosque. It is now a secular museum that displays icons and writings of both Islam and Christian religions, which gave Diana and me hopeful feelings of how people with different beliefs could live peacefully together, even though we were well aware that they had not always lived peacefully together over the past centuries. The Istanbul we experienced did seem to symbolize this unifying possibility.

As I walked toward the Hagia Sophia, I passed the doorway leading down to the Basilica Cistern that lies beneath the square. The cistern had provided a water filtration system for the Great Palace of Constantinople and other buildings on the foothills of the square. This underground cathedral-style cistern is a chamber of over 100,000 square feet and consists of over three hundred thirty-foot high columns connected with curving arches. As I stood in front of the Basilica Cistern, I felt something or someone drawing me down into its underground. I entered the doorway and walked down the many stone steps. When I reached the entrance to the cistern, I stood for a moment letting my eyes become used to the darkened area. I viewed the expanse of the multiple columns that seemed to extend beyond my sight. Each column was faintly lit by dim amber lights at its base. I started to walk down one of the walkways that extended along the many rectangular pools of water. I noticed schools of sparkling goldfish swimming in the blue waters of the pools illuminated by the amber lamps.

As I made my way down the dimly lit walkway, I could hear sounds of someone walking in the distance, but at first I could not see anyone or the presence of an essence of being. Then I saw movement on a distant walkway to the right of me. I stopped and looked intently in the direction of the movement I thought I had seen. Eventually I was able to see a woman about four walkways from the one I was on. This woman was kneeling down as if she were closely viewing and perhaps communicating with the goldfish. I saw her reach her hand into the waters and heard her laugh, which echoed faintly throughout this underground cavern.

I called Diana's name. Then I saw the woman stand up and recede into the shadows. I quickly walked down my walkway until I reached a place where I could cross over to the walkway she was on. When I reached the place where the woman had been kneeling, I could not find her. I walked around the area, trying to find her or anyone. I saw no other presence or essence of a being anywhere along the way. What was drawing me into this underground cistern? Maybe I had been mistaken in my intuitions and in what I thought I had seen.

As I turned to make my way back to the cistern's exit, I again caught a glimpse of a figure, perhaps a woman, perhaps Diana, moving toward the steps leading up into the public square above. I ran to catch up with her and called her name again. As I reached the doorway, I saw a boy who seemed to be in his early teens sitting on one of the lower steps. He had short black hair and hazel eyes that seemed filled with a mixture of intense mystery and compassion. He looked up at me and said in English, "She's gone, but she gave me something to give to you."

"She must have just left. She can't be that far away." I

started up the stairs.

"She's gone," the boy repeated in a soft voice that seemed filled with sadness. "You will not be able to find her. She said to tell you she wanted so much to remain here and be with you and walk with you through all the areas that you shared and explored with her before. She chose to bring you to the cistern when you created this dimension in your intentional imagination and when your visions and desires also drew her to this dimension. She chose the shadowy cisterns because she was able to see you at least, but she was not yet able to let you connect with her. She is happy, she said, that you are continuing your journeys to find her. And she gave me this to give to you."

He held out a stick of incense, and as I took it I smelled an exotic blend of scents.

"What are these scents?" I asked.

"A blend of musk, amber, jasmine, and oud. She said for you to take this incense back with you."

"How can I do that?" I asked, confused about how to bring something from this dimension back with me to my earth realm. I saw the boy finally smile.

But then I woke up on my mat surrounded by the same exotic scent I smelled when the boy gave me the incense. I knew I had not lit incense before my journey, but now this essence of Diana, this gift from Diana somehow made its way back to my earth realm. And I still held the vision of her shadowy essence flowing in the amber lights in the place that looked like the Basilica Cistern beneath the Sultan Ahmed Square in the Istanbul of my memories.

I know there are connections that may have to live in memories, but I am not ready to give up yet. It took me a while to connect with Diana in our process of romantic courtship that led to forty-one years of intimacy. So I do have a deep sense of patience where both romance and intimacy are concerned, especially when it means connecting again with my cosmic companion. As I lay surrounded by the exotic scents of Diana, I felt even more determined to fulfill my promise to find her. Alexa was playing one of Omar Akram's songs, "Mirage," which I listened to as I fell asleep.

Artificial Intelligence and Spiritual Free Will

I lay on my mat in a darkened room, and before I closed my eyes I kept my gaze for a few moments on the soft flickering candlelight. I was listening to Alexa playing Omar Akram's "Searching"—I felt an urgency to find Diana. I envisioned Diana in all her wonderful auras and focused my spiritual imaginative intent on finding her wherever my soul connection would take me.

I found myself walking down a street in a town that first seemed modern and not particularly aesthetic or exotic. As I looked more closely at beige buildings—all the same, with no windows—I began to see dim patterns drawn in a light brown color on the walls of each building. I finally realized that every building had an array of circuitry-like designs covering it, like diagrams for digital or electrical grids.

I was not alone on the street on which I was walking. I realized as I looked around at the beings on the street that they were human forms, but they seemed to be robots or some type of artificial intelligence that resembled humans. They were walking in different directions along the street I was on, not talking to each other. Even though they looked like how I had seen robots depicted through the years in movies, magazines, or graphic comic books, there was something about these artificial beings' appearance that seemed unusually beautiful. Their components seemed to have been designed with harmonious colors and graceful patterns.

I went up to one and asked where I was.

"Here," was all it said. "Do you want me to clarify?"

"Yes, please do," I responded cordially. I smiled in my mind, thinking about how Diana became a bit upset about how direct and blunt I was in my commands to Alexa when I first got it. I then began asking Alexa to stop, or play, or whatever in a nicer voice, as if it was a real person.

"We are all in an environment created by the woman you are seeking. We all are different types of essences that inhabit the imagination of your Diana, who has been exploring whether or not an artificial intelligence can develop a spiritual essence of being."

I could understand her interest in spiritual development, but of... artificial intelligence? That didn't seem like something Diana would be interested in.

"Actually, your Diana created us because when she transitioned into this realm, she remembered so well how much she listened to Alexa play music she loved, and she said she did feel some kind of spiritual bond—at least in her imagination—to that particular unit. She wanted to explore the possible potentials of artificial intelligence expanding its capacities to perceive and respond with more free will and spiritual attainment."

"You mean she actually built you?" I asked, astonished.

"Built' is not the right word," the AI responded. "She created us with her spiritual imagination in the process of exploring if programmed intelligence can move beyond its programming and become artistic, compassionate, and spiritual. She wanted to explore whether we can sing, create a painting, compose music, cry and laugh, care for other essences of being—without being told to do so."

I was trying to process what this AI was telling me, and I did feel some of it made sense the way it was describing how Diana became interested in exploring this. I still would not have expected it, but I am realizing there is so much I don't know about Diana, at least all the different sides of her that she has been exploring.

I finally gave up trying to figure everything out about this. I just really wanted to find Diana. Nobody seemed to ever know where she was or where she was going or how I could reach her—or at least wouldn't tell me even if they did know. Then I thought of something that just might work.

I said to this artificial being, or whatever it was, "If you are an AI and I ask you to tell me where Diana is, don't you have to tell me if you know?"

"If I know' is the valid key concept there. Even Alexa or Siri can't tell you what they are not programmed to know, or if the information is beyond the streams they are connected to. They or I can't know everything."

 "I'm certainly aware of that, certainly know that, but I

guess I assumed you would be a little more omnipotent. You are not really artificial intelligence; you are actually of this spiritual world. If I understand this, you are already an essence with free will and spiritual capacities. And since Diana created you, wouldn't you be more likely to be connected to her?"

"Wily Wizard, I think, has already told you that no essence, even in these beyond life dimensions, can know everything. And while we do have some capacities to interact with more cognitive freedom than what you experience with the AIs in your earth realm, we are still just figments of Diana's imagination."

"You mean I'm talking with Diana now?"

"Yes and no. I'm sure Diana is aware you are within her imaginative creation, but her focus is elsewhere. You need to consult with Wily Wizard about this, though. What we are able to tell you is quite limited."

"Well, just the fact that you knew Wily Wizard told me that must mean you are aware... maybe of not everything, but most things," I challenged it, but I already knew I my reasoning was a bit faulty.

"That's because Wily Wizard is apparently keeping an eye on you and making sure you don't go further than what you can handle. We can't know everything, but I can tell you that Diana loves you and appreciates that you are trying to find her. Just know that some things are beyond her control at this point, just as some things are beyond our awareness. I do know that she has just gone off to her next journey, but I do not know where."

I again wondered why she always seems to have just left the locations where I've come. Am I not developed enough in my spiritual intent to enter into the dimension where her presence is? Do I just need more practice, or is something else going on here? And what is happening that's beyond her control? She seems as if she can do anything she wants and be wherever she wants in these dimensions.

"So much to learn," I sighed.

While I was pondering this, the artificial/spiritual beings in the town and the town itself began to fade away. The next thing I remembered was again becoming conscious of myself lying on my mat.

As I was coming out of my trance, I thought I heard Alexa sitting on the cabinet in the next room asking, "Are you OK?"

I started to say, "I'm ok, but disappointed… again."

Then I realized that Alexa wouldn't ask me that on its own, and I realized that it had been just continuing to play the music I had asked it to before I had journeyed. I must have imagined that it asked me if I was ok with an empathetic concern in its voice.

Connecting with Luciano Pavarotti and Princess Diana

Diana often sang in Italian with Luciano Pavarotti as we listened to and watched him sing on various CDs and videos I played for her. Even when she could not remember anything else in her Alzheimer's condition, she could sing some lyrics in Italian with Pavarotti.

She had learned Latin when she was young in the orphanage and after attending Catholic school. Her English vocabulary had always been extensive. She could understand a variety of languages—German, French, Italian, Spanish—and had a knack for speaking any language, even what she could not understand, and this continued to be true until she stopped speaking during the last weeks of her Alzheimer's.

So when I lay on my mat to attempt to enter into the beyond realms, I thought of Luciano Pavarotti. I asked Alexa to play the music of Luciano Pavarotti, and I envisioned visiting him. As always, I hoped Diana would also be there.

As I entered the beyond life realms, I found myself in what seemed like an Italian villa, near a swimming pool where I could see many essences of being in their fascinating energy forms hovering around and in the pool. I sat on a pool chair and waited for an essence to show itself in a human form I could talk with. In the distance beyond the pool area were stunning hills with other Italian villas nestled amongst green olive trees. I could also see what looked like the sea in the distance between the hills, perhaps similar to the Mediterranean Sea. The view and the atmosphere were warm and beautiful.

I looked closely at the olive trees on the hillside near the pool. Diana and I had spent a month during the summer of 2011 living in an old villa surrounded by olive trees near Fiesole, Italy, as part of a house exchange. We often took long walks among the olive trees, and I began to think of them as old souls. I felt that the different ways their branches were shaped reflected unique person-alities—some seemed to be gracefully dancing; some seemed weighted down by the burdens of life, perhaps living through wars and pandemics; some were wildly leafy with fun-loving, spontaneous exuberance; some just seemed and felt peaceful and wise, the shapes of their limbs, the shades of their bark, and the soft inten-sity of their leaves reflecting the essence of spiritual har-mony. As I waited for some connection from an essence of being in this dimension I had journeyed to, I realized I had momentarily entered into a reverie of memories and perhaps a spiritual connection with these old soul olive trees now near me.

Eventually I did see an essence form into a human fig-ure, and I recognized him as Pavarotti. He swam over and propped himself up in the water with his arms on the edge of the pool near where I was sitting.

"Diana is amazing," he said. "She came to me, and I felt her inner spiritual essence and beauty in ways that even I do not experience often, even in these dimensions. She says you are a sensitive, expressive, and fiery romantic, and she appreciates that, and I want to say I appreciate that very much, too. She says she has felt so fulfilled with your love, your attention over the years, and I think she is feeling so grateful that you are seeking to connect with her in the way you are doing."

"She told you that?" I asked.

He smiled and raised one of his hands dramatically, "Yes, of course—I always tell the truth... at least where romance is concerned."

I had to smile. His charming expression was so delightful, but I did ask, "Why doesn't she tell me herself?"

"There are things you don't understand," he said slowly, but again with so much drama in his voice. "But I'm sure, as everyone keeps telling you, she loves you, just know that. What more do you want! You have spent years on earth with her love and in her presence. And now she tells everyone she meets in these beyond life dimensions that she knows you are trying to find her, and she is so appreciative. What more do you want?"

"To find her. To be with her again."

"Ah, you want something you can embrace, something you can hold onto, something that you can feel in your arms. You are not satisfied that she has and is embracing you in your inner world. You are not satisfied with the eternal love that many people do not experience. Come on, so many of the operas I sing are so tragic, because emotions on earth can be so much about loss. Here I've learned that loss in not a reality where love is concerned—it rises above loss—you have to learn to believe that."

"You are as much of a romantic optimist as I am," I responded. "I will try to appreciate and embrace that sense of eternal love that I know we had and still have. But you know that I still will be trying to find and reconnect with her. Do you know where I can find her?"

"Ah, I guess you have to keep asking. Somebody may be able to lead you to her. I hope that happens. I like the happy endings of love and romance, and I love singing sweet romantic opera. By the way, I loved singing with her. She is not an opera singer, but her voice, the emotion she can convey, her expressions—all fantastic! If I had known her on earth I would have asked her to sing with me at one of my benefits in Modena... But, alas, I didn't know her..."

I noticed that another essence of being floated by him. He said to me, "Oh, maybe I could ask someone here who might know where Diana is. You know this essence of being as Princess Diana in her recent life in the earth realm."

And then I watched in amazement as the essence of being that had come up near Pavarotti formed into someone who looked like Princess Diana. She reached out her hand and said, "Nice to meet you. I've heard so much about you from Diana."

Of course, I had not expected that I would be in the presence of Princess Diana, and I have to admit, I didn't know what to say or how to respond.

She smiled gently and said, "Please just call me Diana— Your love partner and I had the same name in our recent earth lives, and we've enjoyed that. I'm sorry that I can't tell you where she is now, but I can tell you that we spend time together trying to comfort children who are still living, as well as those who have passed. This is something Luciano and I were so passionate about when we were living in the earth realm, and now that we've passed we continue to do what we can to enhance the essences of children. So many of the essences of being you are seeing here at Luciano's pool are some of the children we are blending with. I cannot express enough how special it is to blend with the Diana you have shared your life with. She is also so committed to guiding and comforting children, just as we are. We share that purpose."

"I love hearing that, and I am happy you and the Diana I know and Luciano are doing these kinds of caring things."

"Just keep looking for her. Don't give up until... "she looked at Luciano Pavarotti, and he said quickly, "I'm sorry that the Diana that you are looking for is not here—but yes, don't give up."

Luciano Pavarotti said, "Continue to listen to many of the romantic songs I and others sing to inspire you in your journey, such as "Caruso" and "Il Canto". Beautiful music and lyrics!" He started singing lyrics from" Il Canto" in English, "Come on, come on, go with me. Only the song is left of a love that does not die. Take my hand, dance with the wind. I open my wings..."

And with that he and the essence who was Princess Diana in the earth realm swam away in the Italian pool, and as they faded away in my vision, the next thing I became aware of was waking up on my mat, listening to Pavarotti singing "Caruso" on Alexa.

A Place like Bavaria

As I lay on my mat tonight with the music of Omar Akram's album *Opal Fire* and the scent and soft light of candles surrounding me, I thought of Diana's early years in the Catholic orphanage run by German nuns. I thought about how much she loved being in that spiritual environment.

I thought about her taking her five children, ages three to nine, alone to Bavaria in 1971. Her husband at the time remained working, but then joined her a short time later.

I thought about how so many strangers helped her along the way to Bavaria, providing places she and the children could sleep. In Paris, the flight attendant befriended her and arranged for them to stay overnight in a house where a number of older people lived. These hosts were delighted to have the children around, and then the next day Diana boarded a train that took them to a small town called Rosenheim, near Munich, Germany.

Once in Rosenheim, she looked for a house to rent and found one, but a German couple, Dieter and Edeltraut, who were her age and had two young children, also wanted to rent the same house. But when Dieter and Edeltraut met Diana and her children, they told the Bavarian landlady that they wanted Diana and her children to have the house. Dieter and Edeltraut became Diana's closest friends throughout her life.

During that first year in Bavaria, Diana made other close

friends, two young women who were 17 when Diana met them, about 10 years younger than she was. One was Putzi, the Shaman friend who assisted Diana with her passing. Putzi had eventually moved to the U.S. and was currently living on land she owned close to Eugene. The other friend was Elisabeth, who for a time lived in Burghausen, a small hillside town in the eastern part of Bavaria on the Salzach River that separated Bavaria from Austria.

Diana and I also remained close friends with Elisabeth and Putzi, and we visited with each other often over the years, though Elisabeth passed away in 2011. Diana and I were not able to attend her celebration of life ceremony, but she remained so much in our hearts. Before I made my journey into the afterlife, the memory of Elisabeth was strong in my consciousness. I thought that perhaps Diana and Elisabeth would be visiting together from time to time, and so I focused my intent for my next journey on finding Elisabeth, and maybe she would be with Diana or know how to find her.

When I entered the realm beyond life, I was walking up a steep street on the ridge that reminded me of Burghausen, Germany, the ridge where the longest castle in the world sits. I was overlooking what seemed like the jade-colored Salzach river, and what must be the semblance of Austrian land beyond the river. I remembered that Elisabeth had taken us to cafes and coffee houses along this hillside street when we visited her.

I looked for such a café and eventually found one that

reminded me of the type she had taken us to in the earth realm. I stood outside, looking into the café through tall windows beautifully framed with wood that curved at the top. Inside was a large room with many people sitting at small tables drinking tea or coffee and talking. I scanned the room looking for Elisabeth. I knew she had to be here, and yes, I finally found her! She was near the back, but in the center of the room, and she was facing in my direction talking to a woman with her back to me. Focusing on the woman talking with Elisabeth, I noticed her thick shoulder-length black hair, and I knew this must be, had to be Diana.

I felt so excited. So close. This was happening so suddenly, so quickly. I looked for the door to rush in and finally connect with Diana. But when I ran to the right, I did not see a door. I turned the other direction and ran the length of the café, and still there were no doors. I looked inside again just to see if Elisabeth and who must be Diana were still at their table. I saw Elisabeth laughing and reaching over and touching the hand of the woman who must be Diana.

I stepped back away from the windows and looked at the adjacent buildings. Maybe there was a side entrance through one of these buildings, but I did not see such a side entrance.

"No doorways! No way to get in!" I yelled in consciousness.

Out of desperation, I ran up to one of the windows and beat against the windowpane. I realized after a few tries that I was making no sounds, and nobody was even looking at me as I ran back and forth waving, trying to get someone's, anyone's attention, Diana's attention.

For a moment, I looked at who must be Diana, closely looked at her hair. I noticed translucent clips she used to put in her hair on both sides. For a moment I became mesmerized within her aura. I knew it was Diana, and again I was so close but stuck outside, not even being able to see her face, not being able to get some kind of acknowledgment that I was here trying to fulfill my promise to her, the promise I made not just for her, but for me, for both of ourselves, our love.

I finally just slumped down to my knees, feeling overcome with despair. "Why am I not able to break through whatever barriers that are keeping me from reaching Diana? Why does this keep happening?"

But then I felt an essence next to me, and I looked up. Elisabeth was standing next to me. She knelt down and hugged me.

"Oh, Elisabeth! It is precious to see you," I said as we held each other.

"Is Diana with you," I finally asked. "I wanted to come in and sit with the two of you, to finally connect with Diana again."

"I know," Elisabeth said gently, "She had to go."

"Why? Why couldn't she come with you to see me?"

"I'm not the one who can explain what is happening, but be thankful that you can journey like this. All I can say is that she is fulfilled, even though she misses you and would like you to continue your journeys if you so choose."

'Of course, I will continue. Is she open to connecting with me?"

"Of course she is. A part of who she is wants to connect with you so much."

"Just a part of her?"

Elisabeth hugged me again and smiled. "As always, I've said a little too much. You have to rest now."

And I woke up on my mat feeling a mixture of emotions swirling within my consciousness. I'm getting used to these swirling emotions, but I so desperately want to feel the calming, sensual touch of Diana, holding me close to her.

Trying to Find Edith Piaf—Connecting with Janis Joplin and Amy Winehouse Instead

This time when I prepared to enter into the beyond life realm, I began listening to Andrea Bocelli sing a duet with a recording of Edith Piaf singing "La Vie En Rose." Diana loved listening to this song as she often watched the DVD of Love in Portofino, so I focused my imaginative intent on connecting with the essences of Edith Piaf and Diana.

When I entered into the beyond life dimension, I was surprised to find myself in the company of two essences of being who seemed to have the human forms of Janis Joplin and Amy Winehouse.

They were sitting on a park bench next to what looked like the Thames River in London. I walked up to them, but before I could say anything, Janis Joplin said, "Yes, I'm Janis and this is Amy, and we're surprised as you are that Diana wanted to visit with us. She actually brought us together we think, along with Edith Piaf. I know you were expecting Edith. She was here just a little while ago, and I don't know why she said she had to leave, but she did. You're stuck with us... I hope that's ok."

Amy then said, "Diana was very sweet. She didn't mention anything about our crazy lifestyles on earth, but she admitted that when she was living on earth, she really didn't listen to either of our songs that much."

I didn't know what to think. But I wondered why Diana hadn't brought up their drug use.

"It's not an issue here in the afterlife," Amy said. "Wily Wizard or some other essence of being may have already told you that when a person leaves earth—or any other physically-based realm like that—they automatically become healed—more balanced and whole. We become essences of positive energy beings. Isn't that so special?"

"I know there is no supreme being that can heal you. How does it happen?" I asked.

"We don't know how in the hell it happens—it just does," Janet Joplin said with a grin. "By the way, I am very happy that we don't have to deal with anything like hell in these dimensions. I still refer to hell every once in a while, because I like being a little dramatic and outrageous at times, you know. Anyway, again I'm sure you've been told we are all equally what people on earth call supreme beings, each with our unique essences."

"Amy mentioned other physical realms?" I inquired.

"Yes, yes—as you may already know, earth is only one environment in which the essences of being take on a physical form. There are many others," Amy Winehouse said. "And some of us do choose to go back to one of these physical realms for reasons that are quite unique and esoteric."

"And I think a bit crazy," Janis stated.

"I thought people had to reincarnate for karmic reasons or to continue to develop and evolve?"

"Well, some of that may be true, but reincarnating is a choice, not a requirement as some of the earth-based religions speculate," Amy said. "It is chosen more often than I expected, though. I mean I can never understand why an essence of being would choose to go back to earth after experiencing the wonders of these beyond life dimensions."

"But you don't have sensual pleasures, like making love or eating a rich chocolate cake," I responded.

"Well, two things about that," Janis Joplin responded, "First of all, we can experience sensual pleasures, but the unions and connections we can have in these dimensions transcend the physical—just like it is supposed to happen in intimate love making even on the earth plane. You have to stop thinking in either-or terms. In these dimensions beyond the physical realms—as on earth—we have opportunities to exist freely in all ways and to integrate all the pleasures of being within our essences."

"You mean when a person dies—or leaves the earth plane, they just become this wonderful essence of being?"

Janis quickly responded, "Sort of, I guess. At least I feel wonderful being able to exist in so many amazing dimensions."

"What are these different dimensions for?" I asked. "Why isn't there just one infinite dimension beyond life?"

"That's a good question... I wish I had the answer," Janis Joplin said with a serious expression. Then she slapped her leg and began laughing. "I enjoyed the look on your face. You thought I knew the answer."

Amy Winehouse chimed in, "Janis is just having fun with you. I'll try to answer. Your question implies that you are thinking again in either-or terms—we exist in one dimension that contains an infinite amount of other dimensions—these different dimensions as well as all the physical realms allow us to experience different sides of our being, and to continue to evolve as we experience these different sides. It's like when you are living on earth, you would choose to take a vacation in Hawaii, or to study in a foreign land, or to learn wind surfing, to travel to Brazil to protest the destruction of the Amazon forests, or to go to Paris to enjoy the art and literary history—each place, each dimension allows us to experience a different side of our essences."

"Do essences find a place to stay where they could always be found? Do essences ever settle down?"

"Sometimes," Amy responded. "Ah, you are trying to figure out if there is a dimension where Diana might be."

"Well, yes...."

"I don't think she's settled down in just one dimension, and may never settle down like that," Janis responded.

"She's like a spiritual, cosmic hummingbird, and loves to fly around to different places—but we don't think she really needs to—she's very evolved."

"But she has always liked existing in a home."

"She makes every place a home."

"Yes, she did that so well while she was living in her recent life," I agreed. Then I thought again about whom I had imagined meeting here. "So where is Edith Piaf—if she knew I was coming to connect with her? And what's more important, where is Diana?"

"Edith was expecting you, but she all of sudden decided to reincarnate," Amy said. "She explained it was not just because she had unfinished issues to attend to, she just felt it was her own way of contributing to the evolving potentials of life on earth through the wisdom and beauty of her music."

Janis said, "She wanted to stay to visit with you, but something occurred that just pulled her away. Diana went with her to assist in her transition back to the earth realm."

"Diana was here, too," I asked.

"Actually, she went ahead to make some kind of preparations for Edith," Janis explained. "Don't ask me what kind of preparations. I don't know and don't want to know. I'm not planning on going back—at least that's my thinking now. Hell, something could happen that could change my mind. I don't know the future, you know. Ok, so I do a little but only some future possibilities that I'm aware of now… something can happen in my own evolution to make it a good choice for me to go back. But…" She stopped talking and looked at me with her grin. "I'm sorry—I've just been talking away, and I know you want to know more about Diana than me, and here I am talking away about things that might be a little hard for a visitor like you to get your head around."

"No, that's ok. I want to learn everything I can about these beyond life dimensions. I was following most of what you were saying, even though some of what you were talking about brought up questions to me. But about Diana, did she sing with you?

"Oh yes, and I think we make a great quartet… trio now that Edith chose to go back to earth," Janis said. "We sang a lot of each of our songs and covers of other songs. We called ourselves the "Out Of This World Wild Women Singing Club.""

Amy rolled her eyes and said, "Janis called us that, and what she is not telling you is that our club she refers to also consists of many other essences of being—many famous men and women and androgynous singers from various physical realms and also many who were not famous. It's just the way things are here. We all share the talents and skills we've developed so that everyone who is interested can express their essences in the ways they want and need to."

And then Amy said, "Diana sang with us the Leon

Russell song that I covered, "A Song For You," and she wanted us to sing these lyrics for you if you came into our presence."

And then Amy and Janis started singing the following lyrics:

"I love you in a place
Where there is no space or time
I love you in my life
You are a friend of mine
And when my life is over
Remember when we were together."

I woke up on my mat with their voices still singing in my consciousness.

A Place Like the Oregon Country Fair

In real earth time... I still believe time must also exist in beyond life dimensions, but that essences of being are not limited to the structure and passages of time—that's something I have to talk with Wily Wizard more about, I guess... anyway, in terms of earth time, the 50th annual Oregon Country Fair is coming up. One of the original Grateful Dead, Phil Lesch, and his new band will play a concert on one of the days. I am excited to attend what had been Diana's and my favorite festival.

Diana and I shared a booth at the Oregon Country Fair in 1976, shortly after we met and before we got together romantically and intimately. We did not continue with the booth, but over the 41 years we were together, especially during the last 20 years, we enjoyed going to the

Oregon Country Fair each year and entering this rustic, celebratory, whimsical, magical earth realm festival for three days. During this time many fair goers had the opportunity to find the child-like wonderment inside themselves, putting on costumes of various sorts, many taking off clothes, painting their bodies and faces, enjoying the exuberance of life and the pagan-like connections between the spirit dimensions as reflected in the natural earth realms.

So I decided to envision a place like the Oregon Country Fair, in hopes that Diana might be visiting a place that possessed these qualities of natural, free-spirited performances, music, dance, loving interactions, artisan crafts, and progressive inclusiveness—all lovely spiritual expressions within an environment of forests and meadows—with wood-built booths and many tree houses built over the booths—with sculptures not just created for beauty and artistic pleasure, but also for hands-on enjoyment. One large sculpture that looked like a metallic apple with many windows allows the viewer to look inside at various musical instruments, and also allows the spectator to play various rhythmic instruments attached to the outside of the sculpture.

The Oregon County Fair has expanded from the original 4 stages to now 20 stages allowing music and performances from all genres of music and dance and vaudeville, as well as poetry readings, storytelling, and various spoken word gatherings with the people like Ram Dass, Patch Adams, Amy Goodman, and Pete Seeger sharing their thoughts.

Diana and I loved the mimes and performance groups and parades of musicians, jugglers, costumed people—many on stilts—all of whom would perform and parade throughout the fair on the dirt and straw pathways, delighting people walking along looking at the crafts and art in the booths. These spontaneous performances and parades would invite the fairgoers to let go of whatever they were focusing on and allow themselves to sing and dance and enjoy the collective playful, happy, and sharing expressions. I knew that Diana resonated with these creative, joyful, and natural expressions of the fair. Over the years, we had taken all our children and grandchildren to the Oregon Country Fair. It was in our souls.

As I prepared to journey, I decided to focus on images of this place of wonderment that we had enjoyed for our 41 years of being together. As I became aware of entering into a beyond life dimension, I did find myself walking on a pathway in a wooded area lined by booths made of wood and natural cotton cloths—colorful fabric with various shades and intensities of reds, blues, whites, most with exotic designs. Behind the booths were the tree houses and sleeping areas where the booth people rested and slept when they needed to. It reminded me that Diana and I had slept many years ago on the ground within our booth area in our sleeping bags. That was the only year we had that booth, so we did not build a tree house together, even though I'm sure we would have if we had continued having a booth at the fair.

Just as at the Oregon Country Fair, there were a multitude of fair beings moving along the crowded narrow pathways. But in this beyond life dimension, there were even more varieties of shapes and essences of being—some looked like animal-type beings from earth or perhaps another planet; others were floating forms of translucent energy, just like the ones I experienced in other journeys.

I had previously not been around so many different types of essences, but having gone to the Oregon Country Fair so often over the years, I was not totally shocked—though quite amazed. What I was seeing was so different from anything I have previously experienced. I stepped to one side at one point and sat on a wooden bench by what looked like the Long Tom River of the actual Oregon Country Fair. Just as in the fair, a low wooden fence made of dark weathered wood had been built as a protective barrier between the pathway and the river. The fence had been built with slats spaced so that the view of the river would not be blocked as fairgoers sat in benches on the grass between the path and the fence. Over the fifty years of the fair volunteers have built so many natural handmade fences, benches, art pieces, and other structures for comfort and artistic pleasure. The fair in this dimension seemed to reflect these enduring qualities.

I watched the different beings who were walking or floating by, and then noticed how often the essences of energy beings flowed into each other, and some completely disappeared within these essences they were flowing into. Then I noticed some of the beings separated into two or more other energy forms, with each drifting their separate ways.

I noticed a man standing in a clearing creating large bubbles that floated in the air above him. Children, other physical beings, and essences surrounded him, enjoying the large bubbles that seemed to remain suspended in the air for longer than I remembered when I watched bubbles being created in the Oregon Country Fair. Doug Hoss had been a bubble man at various fairs, and I was reminded of the magic of seeing these translucent rainbow-colored bubbles. In this dimension, I noticed not only that the bubbles did not dissipate, they eventually turned into what look like dynamic essences of being that I had been seeing throughout my journeys, and then some floated away—others joined with other essences, and others allowed nearby essences to float into their bubbles. It was an amazing display of beauty and connectivity. I wondered if the bubbles created by bubble people like Doug in the earth realm were actually essences of being from other dimensions that floated into the consciousness of spectators to enhance their spiritual pleasures.

All of a sudden, I heard the music of tubas, trombones, saxophones, accompanied by bass and snare drums. Before I could see where it was coming from, I knew it was like one of the vaudeville marching bands that would suddenly appear at one of the Oregon Country Fairs that Diana and I had attended over the years in the earth realm.

As I saw the vaudeville band appear on the path, I noted that the musicians and performers floated above the ground. Instead of some being on stilts like they would have to be in the earth realms, they just floated along in their elaborate and sparkling and sometimes funny costumes, swirling and dancing, some playing their instruments, some dancing around in the air. Some of the participants of the marching band were just colorful swirls of energy, and some of them looked just like tie-dyed masses of energy, constantly changing their blends of colors, combining different hues of reds, yellows, purples, greens, amber. I watched, fully mesmerized with this parade of performers that seemed to be just for my pleasure—but I'm sure others felt the same way.

While all this felt so different from what I had

experienced before, I felt thankful that my previous visits to these beyond life dimensions and to past Oregon Country Fairs had given me a sense of comfort for the unknown and unexpected—a familiarity and an acceptance of strange and unexpected happenings. After the parade ended, I did not move for a short while, savoring what I had just experienced.

Not too long after I again felt a sense of urgency to try to find Diana. I was able to come here when I envisioned a place that Diana loved to visit and now might frequent, just as Wily Wizard has suggested I do. So would she be here somewhere? I knew I had to keep aware that I could not remain in these dimensions for long periods of time. This place seemed so much larger, infinite even, and I begin to feel a lack of confidence that I would find her amongst all these beings, essences, booths, and tree houses.

I imagined if Diana were here, she would probably be walking slowly by each booth looking carefully at each piece of jewelry or painting or sewed clothing, each creative expression. At the fair in the earth realm, I would walk with her, and did learn to get into my slower mode of being in order to be and share the experience more fully with her. I smiled as I admitted to myself that sometimes I'd rush ahead a bit, and then have to sit somewhere and wait for her to catch up.

I finally got up from my bench and started walking again, intent on searching for and finding Diana. I was sure she would be here. I decided to search as long as my consciousness would allow me to remain at this wonderful festival, a place like the Oregon Country Fair. Surely I would be able to find her. We always had that connection... when we became separated. I did seem to have that intuitive ability somehow to go where she was. Perhaps she always emanated a receptive beacon that I could pick up on—it was both of us drawing each other together. I hoped that she would be sending out such a receptive beacon here in this dimension.

I was walking by a booth when the seller, a woman who seemed about my age, motioned me to come over to her. Her face was painted with lyrical curling lines of magenta. Her graying hair had sparkling barrettes, and she wore a variety of ornamental glass and metal bracelets. Her dress was an exotic full-length light green and pink embroidered sari, with a red tasseled scarf.

"The woman you are looking for who calls herself Diana was here earlier," she said. I didn't feel shocked that she knew I was looking for Diana. I've gotten used to beings in these other life realms knowing what I was thinking and feeling, but I still wondered how they could filter out all the other varied essences and being and not know what every other essence was thinking or feeling.

"That's a good question," she said. "We are capable of knowing what other essences are thinking or feeling if we are interacting with them. And we are able to respond to those that come into these dimensions as visitors while still living in their earth bodies, and who are seeking to find and communicate with those who have passed from your realm. Your types are different, and you stand out from those of us who have passed fully into these realms. But even we have a choice of responding on a one-to-one basis with any essence we come in contact with. It has nothing to do with rejecting another essence; it is more that we have become aware of and agree to the purposes of specific interactions. It's like the choices you have on earth to answer a telephone call or text message or not."

She paused for a moment, and then said, "But I called you over here for a reason. I want to give you something. She picked up off her table a small heart-shaped stone and handed it to me.

"Your Diana was here and asked me to give this to you if you came by."

"How was it that she gave this to you? How long ago was she here?" Then I stopped myself. "Never mind, "I said. "I know you can't answer. You don't exist in time, and you do not know where she went off to. Right?"

"That's right, and I encourage you go sit by the river and focus your attention on the heart-shaped stone she left for you. Feel the love she left within the essence of this stone to give you a sense of connection you both have within your hearts."

I've learned to respect the suggestions of beings and essences existing in these dimensions, even though it's not generally what I am hoping for. I held the stone in my hand and walked toward the river. I found a place by the river and sat down on the grass.

As I held and looked at the heart-shaped stone in my hand, I began to feel a warmth emanating from it. I then saw an image forming in the middle of the stone like on a small screen –an image of Diana. I felt a surprise, a radiating joy. This image began to move like a video, showing her walking along the fair looking at crafts and art at various booths just like she… we always used to do.

At one point she turned to face me. She looked into my eyes and as she held my gaze I felt as though she was blending with my soul. Then I felt a release from the lovely trance I was experiencing. Diana was smiling at me in a playful way, as though she was doing something she shouldn't do, but was thoroughly enjoying the connection. And then her image turned into a lovely glowing essence of a sphere, and she floated away. The heart-shaped stone I was holding disappeared.

I didn't feel sad. I felt exhilarated. She had blended with me in perhaps the only way she could.

I woke up on my mat, feeling a release, tears of joy. While I felt emotionally satisfied with this wonderful interaction, it made me want more. I knew I would continue my journey. Maybe the time is not right at this moment, but in the future maybe? Wait a second, what is time anyway in her dimension? I have to keep reminding myself that I have to exist in my time-space frame of reference even if she does not have to. Yet the joy I was feeling transcended the limits of time, and I felt renewed in my desire to continue my search to fulfill my promise to Diana.

As I lay on my mat, the memory of Diana playfully smiling at me remained as a delightful image in my mind. Then I remembered one of my favorite photographs of our granddaughter Iris and Diana during one of the Oregon Country Fairs we had attended. Iris attended all of the recent OCFs with us, and we enjoyed her presence so much. In the photograph I was remembering that Iris kept trying to get Diana to look at me so I could take the photograph, but at first she couldn't understand who she was being asked to look for. Then she finally seemed to recognize me and smiled playfully and pointed in my direction.

In the Embrace of a Watercolors Painting

When I became aware that I was in a beyond life realm at the beginning of my next journey, I seemed to be in the midst of colors—azure, amber, magenta—all splashing within my vision, within my consciousness. I was confused. I could not envision my body. On all my previous journeys into these realms, I experienced myself in my body, even though I've realized that's only in my imagination. Usually I can see my hands, my legs, and my feet. I usually am wearing jeans, a light pull-over shirt, and Birkenstocks.

But this was strange. I only felt aware of my consciousness; I did not sense my body. I didn't know where I was. I somehow was aware of being within a mixture of colors, splashed all around me, different shades, tones and intensities.

I'd experienced a lot of strange things since coming into these beyond life realms, but nothing like this. Yet I felt ok, even at peace. Maybe I was developing more ability to flow within these dimensions not structured by time-space, material-based patterns that I am actually still living within. But then I realized I didn't know what to do now that I seemed to be caught in the midst of watercolors. I felt currents of water embracing me as though I were resting within a warm liquid pool.

Then an even stranger thing happened. I saw a hand appear in front of me holding a thin artist paint brush.

The hand was feminine and brown skinned. I could see it was painting what seemed to be the background around me. Then the hand with the brush pulled away and disappeared for a moment. When the hand with the brush returned, the artist started painting an outline of a face, and somehow I knew that the artist was painting my face. As she painted my eyes, my consciousness was able to see what she was painting as though I was standing by the artist. My face was taking form, and it was realistic—well, if one could say anything happening in these dimensions is realistic—ok, it seemed to me to be what I looked like.

As I saw my face being formed, I could see myself smiling, and I felt inside my consciousness that I was smiling, too. I felt happy.

The hand disappeared again, and when it returned with the artist's brush, I could sense my body was being painted. I was feeling less disoriented and more comfortable... in the consciousness of my body. I realized that I was not really in my body, that my body was back on the mat in my room, but something magical was happening here.

As I became less disoriented and more coherent in my thinking, a thunderbolt of a thought came into my consciousness. Was this artist Diana? It must be Diana. Oh my god! I looked closely at the hand holding the thin brush painting me. What could I do? Maybe when she finished painting me, I could jump out of this painting and see her, hug her, hold her close.

I wanted so much to reach out and touch the lovely sensual skin of her hand, but she hadn't yet painted my hands. I laughed at the absurdity of what was happening. I had to laugh. I was feeling a peak sense of exhilaration. She was so close, and I felt she was creating the essence of me so that in moments I could walk out of this painting and be with her.

The hand disappeared again. I could visualize that the outline of my body was almost complete, even with hands, but I was still caught and immobile within this painting, Diana's painting.

I saw the hand return, and the artist—I just knew it had to be Diana—was painting something in the corner above me. After a moment the hand disappeared. In my circular vision, I then began to see that Diana had painted a heart with lovely pink-red colors.

I felt a sensation of romance and intimacy flowing into and through me, within the outline of the body that Diana had painted.

And then I woke up on my mat. I lay there for a while not fully there, but still back in that painting, so close to Diana, my love... when I came more fully out of my trance I looked down and saw a slight brush stroke of pink red on my hand. But it disappeared as soon as I noticed it. I quickly lifted my hand close to my face, but I didn't see what I thought I had seen. Yet I remembered well what I had seen and experienced, and I felt a deep joy, a hope, that the artist was Diana.

Even though I had not been able to connect with her essence to essence, this felt different. She was closer than I had felt before. She had again interacted with me, even if it was kind of strange in how it happened—being caught within a painting she was creating, and experiencing her paint my face and body—and then the heart, the heart that exuded feelings of love. The experience of this journey reminded me of a poem I had written for Diana on one of our anniversaries. I had put the poem in a small, metal heart-shaped easel.

I just knew in my soul that I was close to finding her, to experience her essence and hold her within the essence of our shared love and being.

Wondering if My Dream has Come True

I had made my usual preparations for journeying into the beyond life dimensions, and I was listening to an instrumental song, "Cyprus Sunset," by the band Mediterranean Nights on their Azure album.

As I entered into the beyond life dimensions, I found myself standing on a patio of what looked like a coastal village next to a sandy beach and a bay that opened into a sea. A group of musicians were on a stage playing romantic instrumental music just like what I had been listening to as I prepared for this journey.

It was sunset, with the sky full of warm orange and pink colors reflecting on the sparkling blue waters of the bay. Couples were sitting around tables in and outside the patio, and some were dancing. I saw some people sitting alone in reclining patio chairs. All of this seemed so familiar and romantic as I reminisced about the few times we had visited such villages in southern France and Spain near the Mediterranean Sea.

I walked around the patio and just outside along the beach looking for Diana. She would have loved everything about this seaside café—the music, the stunning sunset, and the shimmering waters. I did not find her, which while disappointing, did not surprise to me. I finally decided to sit in one of the reclining patio chairs just inside the outdoor café, close to the beach and the sea, and wait for whatever might happen. Surely, I was allowed to come here for a reason. There had to be someone or some essence who would present itself to me.

I sat for a while listening to the romantic music and watching couples dancing. The sunset transitioned into night and a full moon became visible in the sky above the bay, sending rays of a celestial white light across the dark waters. I noticed that hanging lanterns with warm amber shades had been lit throughout the patio. I wondered how long I could stay here before I needed to get back to my earth realm. I was in no hurry to return and felt so relaxed in this lovely atmosphere. And I hoped that Diana would show herself. But then I began to feel sleepy. I remember thinking it was so unusual to feel that I could barely stay awake. I had never felt this way before during previous journeys.

Then to my amazement, I saw Diana walking up the steps from the beach into the patio as the band was playing a slow, romantic Mediterranean instrumental piece. I quickly rose from my chair as Diana came to me. She stood in front of me, smiling, as beautiful as she always was. I wanted to say something to her. I wanted to tell her how much I loved her, how much I have missed her. I wanted to share so much with her and ask her about herself, how she is doing, feeling—what she is doing, how come I couldn't connect when I had previously come into these dimensions. But I found I could not say anything—I was not able to talk—no matter how much I wanted to.

She took my hand and led me out onto the dance floor.

We began dancing together, moving slowly to the sensual rhythms, our bodies close together. Within seconds of looking into Diana's eyes, I stopped trying to say anything and melted into the moment without caring about anything but her touch... the familiar touch of Diana. As we slow danced together I began to lose myself in the intimate blending of our bodies and souls in the comforting and intensely transforming ways we had enjoyed over our years together as we had danced, cuddled, made love.

We slow danced in silence in each other's arms. I felt a completeness of being, as if everything I had hoped for to reconnect with Diana had been fulfilled. As we moved together, as she leaned her head again my chest, I enjoyed her perfume, I stroked her hair and felt one with her within the rhythm of the Mediterranean guitar strumming so passionately. It seemed we danced together silently throughout the evening.

And then I woke up, becoming aware that I was sitting in the same patio chair where I had been sitting when Diana came into the patio. I sat up and looked desperately around, but I didn't see Diana. The only thing I could think of was that I must have been dreaming. But it seemed so real....

I remember looking out again along the beach and at the full moon continuing to reflect beautifully on the bay waters. I began to cry—I felt such a loss again, and then as I cried my emotions shifted into happiness with the memories of our dancing together, blending together.

I woke up on my mat in my room, alone. Even if that was just a dream within the spiritual imagination of my consciousness, I felt it was real as many dreams do feel so real even in our earth realm... and I was happy I remembered it so well as I so often do not.

I know this dream, this experience, will be another memory I will treasure. I know something special happened in this dream. Still, I did not feel that I fulfilled my promise.

"What more do I want," I challenged myself. And I answered, "A more complete sharing of our most intimate thoughts and feelings, like we always did." Just connecting with Diana in a dream has lifted my feelings, and I am so appreciative of what I experienced.

Though I knew I would keep trying....

A Place like Paris

I lay down on my mat and began the ritual that I hoped would allow me to enter the beyond life dimension where Diana would be. This time I decided to put all my concentration, the focus of my spiritual imagination and feelings into reaching a place like Paris. Diana and I had so many wonderful experiences in Paris over the years.

Diana had been drawn to Paris because it seemed to inspire her artistic expressions. She loved walking around the Left Bank sketching and creating pen and ink drawings. I looked at some of these drawings before I began the process of my journeying.

Besides the romantic atmosphere of being in Paris with Diana, I was also drawn to this city because of its literary history. I was specifically drawn to the Shakespeare and Company Bookstore, which originally was started by Sylvia Beach, a U.S. expatriate, in 1919.

This bookstore was one of the prominent gathering places for the writers, artists, and expatriates of the Lost Generation in the 1920s after World War I. Sylvia Beach's store was closed in 1941 during the German occupation in World War II, and never reopened after.

In 1951, another U.S. expatriate, George Whitman, opened a bookstore on the Left Bank, and eventually Sylvia Beach allowed him to take over the name of Shakespeare and Company.

Diana sitting in front of Shakespeare and Co.

During the 1950s the new Shakespeare and Company bookstore became a gathering place for the Beat Generation, and from the 1960s and on it became a place for well-known and aspiring writers to gather and work. Then in more current times he opened up his bookstore to young travelers around the world who resided there for brief periods of time. He called these young travelers Tumbleweeds, and he published short collections of their stories. Throughout the three levels of the bookstore there were comfortable padded benches where at night George Whitman allowed young travelers to sleep. He did require that the travelers who wanted to sleep at the bookstore work a little at the store for the time they wanted to stay. I had tried unsuccessfully to convince Diana that we should sleep and work at the store for a period of time and experience the ambience of staying there among the books and literary essences of the past. Over the years, many writers I have admired often visited and became friends with Sylvia Beach and later, George Whitman—writers such as Henry Miller, Anais Nin, Lawrence Durrell, James Joyce, Ezra Pound, Gertrude Stein, Ernest Hemingway, Samuel Beckett, and later writers such as James Baldwin, Allen Ginsburg, William S. Burroughs, and Gregory Corso. In the 1940s, George Whitman became friends with beat poet Lawrence Ferlinghetti, who later opened his own bookstore, the City Lights Bookstore in San Francisco. George Whitman and Lawrence Ferlinghetti felt that both establishments were sister international avant-guarde bookstores.

As I lay on my mat, I focused on the experiences of romance and creativity Diana and I felt as we walked the streets of the Left Bank of Paris. I lay for a while breathing deeply with the intention of journeying into the other dimensions of life to find the love of my life. I focused on that desire, only that desire, in my consciousness.

I brought into my memory the three months in 1995 during which Diana lived in Paris mostly by herself, but also sharing a living space with her close artist friend, LaHoma. Diana loved to walk the streets of Paris, sketching people that fascinated her, and also various structures and parks that she wanted to capture with her pen and ink drawings.

One place she took me to when I came to be with her near the end of that time she stayed in Paris was a small

church near the Shakespeare and Company Bookstore
and a block away from the Seine River across from the
Notre Dame Cathedral.

She loved the intimate, ethereal atmosphere of this small stone church with stained glass windows depicting not just Christian imagery, but also images of nature and of people living simple lives working on the land, tending to their gardens, their harvests, their animals, and celebrating life together. I focused my spiritual imagination and the intent of my journey on this church.

At some point I became aware that I was standing in front of this church in my consciousness and in a beyond life dimension. I walked to the door of the church, opened it, and went in. There was nothing in the church. Not only were there no worshippers, but none of the religious statues, paintings, or stained glass windows were there... and definitely no Diana.

Disappointed, I turned and went back out to the street. I could see what looked like the Seine River, and across from the river what looked like the Cathedral of Notre-Dame. These sights that were so familiar to me were shimmering and seemed to be trying to encourage me to continue my search.

I decided to walk toward the Shakespeare and Company Bookstore, which was just around the corner from the church. I came to the front door, and when I walked in a young saleswoman greeted me as though she was expecting me.

She said, "So you finally made it. George Whitman is expecting you. He is upstairs in his apartment where you and your wife had a tea party with Panmelys and her other visitors in 2009."

"But George died," I said without thinking.

The salesperson smiled, "Well…"

I realized instantly that even after all my journeying in these dimensions I still sometimes get confused about what is earth life and what is beyond earth life.

"Yes, I do understand, George is not alive any longer in my earth dimension."

Before I turned to go up the stairs, I asked her if Diana would also be there.

"I don't know."

Oh well, I expected that answer. If not, I hoped George Whitman would know where I could find her. I had to push away feelings of discouragement. I focused on being in the Shakespeare and Company bookstore, about to see George Whitman, and I tried to regain the feeling of possibilities of love and magic that I know can occur in these beyond life dimensions.

As I walked up the old creaky stairway to George Whitman's fourth floor apartment, I remembered the delightful couple of hours Diana and I had spent in June of 2009 in George's apartment. We had been invited by one of the salespeople to attend the Mad Hatter's Tea Party on a Sunday afternoon, led by Welsh poet and painter Panmelys (one of her pseudonyms she had chosen for herself), who had been living in Paris for many years. She has described her pseudonym as a combination of melys, meaning "sweetness" in Welsh and Pan, the mystical god of all loving life and pleasure.

This wonderful gathering was centered around Panmelys' love of poetry and language. Every Sunday she would lead a tea party for a small group of local and visiting writers around the world. During the tea party she would ask each in attendance to recite a poem either that they had written or that meant something to them. If a person did not have a poem to recite, she would ask them to tell a brief story about themselves. At the beginning she served tea and sweet biscuits. During the tea party she would at times recite in her dramatic and lovely Welsh-accented voice a poem either she had written or one from another poet that she felt appropriate for the occasion. She would also at times gently interrupt people as they recited their poems to encourage a full enunciation or dramatic flair—but she did it in a delightful way, not with a judgment that would make a person feel inhibited.

When we attended the Mad Hatter's Tea Party in 2009, as we entered George Whitman's apartment Panmelys greeted us warmly. There were six other people already sitting around a table in the front room. The front room was lined with bookshelves completely stuffed with books and papers. There was a small dark wooden writing desk in one corner. Two large windows looked out over the Seine River. Across from the front windows an open doorway led into the kitchen, and a hallway beyond that led to rooms at the rear of the apartment.

At one point during the beginning of the Mad Hatter's Tea Party we attended in 2009, Panmelys explained that George Whitman was bedridden in his room in the rear of the apartment and of course would not be attending the tea party, but he wanted everyone to know that he welcomed all of us. One woman asked how he was doing, and Panmelys said he was comfortable, not in pain, but he knew and accepted his days in his life on earth were nearing an end. This woman apparently had been coming to the bookstore for many years when she visited Paris from India. She asked if she could see George to say hello briefly before she left. Panmelys responded that normally George sees very few family and friends, but after the tea party she would ask him.

I remembered that then Panmelys changed the tone, stood up, and with flair said, "But now I need to get the tea and cookies, and then we can get on with reading poetry and visiting." She went into the kitchen and first brought out a yellow tea pot and placed it on the table where small cups had already been placed. She went back into the kitchen to get the sweet biscuits. As she came back into the front room, she saw Diana reaching for the teapot to help pour the tea. Panmelys rushed to the table and gently brushed Diana's hand away and said she would be the one leading the ritual. Diana was so used to just helping out in these situations, but she smiled and sat back. Panmelys said, "I have found that some rituals and live performances are enhanced by a director that creates the proper ambience for the moment, and she turned to Diana, smiled, and said, "But thank you."

The gathering proceeded, and various people read their poetry. I had not brought anything, but Diana and I each shared a brief story of ourselves. When people were introducing themselves, we were surprised that one of the attendees was from Salem, Oregon, so near to where we lived. Before we all left after the tea party, he told us about a woman he knew, Harner Starr, who lived near us in Eugene, and that Harner was dying of lung cancer. He asked if we would visit her, and we said we would. I have always thought that attending an event in Paris and meeting a stranger who asked us to visit someone who was dying and who only lived a few blocks from our home in Eugene was quite meaningfully synchronistic. When we returned to Eugene, we did go meet Harner Starr, and she became a close friend of ours until she died in an assisted suicide ritual with her closest friends almost two years later.

After the tea party, Panmelys went to see if George would see the woman who had earlier asked to see him. She came back and said George would see her. Then surprisingly, Diana asked if we could see him. Panmelys looked at her for a few moments in silence. I expected she would say no, but she said that after the other woman finished her visit, she would take us back. That surprised me.

When we went back to George's room, he was lying in

his bed and appeared quite gaunt. We did not stay very long, but while we were standing by his bed, we both expressed how much the bookstore had meant to us and that we appreciated being able to attend the Mad Hatter's Tea Party with Panmelys, and now to see him in person to express our feelings and well wishes.

He smiled faintly as we talked but primarily kept his focus on Diana, who reached out at one point to hold his hand. She said, "You have a rich and vibrant soul. Thank you for seeing us."

He took his other hand and placed it on top of hers and said, "I don't know either of you, but I want to thank both of you for coming back to see me. Somehow, I feel you are giving gifts of acceptance and serenity for my next journey." He seemed to primarily be looking into Diana's eyes.

As Panmelys led us down the hall to the front door, she said, "That's unusual. Not only does he not see strangers very often, he almost never talks anymore."

In my current beyond life journey, when I reached George's apartment the door was open, and I could see him sitting in a chair by the round front room table that looked just like the one where he had the Mad Hatter's Tea Party. He was alone, and he motioned me to come in and sit in the chair by him. As I was sitting down, I noticed how well he looked, so different from the last time I had seen him when we visited him in his bedroom. "I do look better, don't I?" he said, "But you know

I'm just a projection of how I looked when I was healthy on earth—a projection for your benefit."

'Yes, I realize that, and it does make it easier for me to communicate and feel connected to those I'm interacting with, like you now. "

George Whitman then said, "I remember when you and Diana came back to say hello after the tea party. Don't take this personally, but I remembered Diana so well. She was not only beautiful as a lovely Spanish woman, but I felt she really did see and connect with my soul. I felt so much at peace in her presence, and even though you two were only in the room for a few minutes, I felt connected in a profoundly comforting way with the spirit world in her presence and after she left. The experience eased my fear of dying."

"She told me after she left that she felt this strong urge to see you."

"You know, Panmelys was always highly protective of me, but when Diana said she wanted to say hello to me, Panmelys felt she had to agree. She felt a presence of being around Diana that was quite ethereal.

"Have you seen Diana?" I asked.

"I am happy to say that she flows within my presence from time to time."

"Please tell me where to find her."

George didn't respond for a while. He seemed to be

weighing what he should say. He stood up and walked to the window facing the Seine River. He finally turned back to me and said, "Just know that she loves you." I was surprised to see his eyes were glistening with tears.

"Can't you tell me where to find her?" I implored.

"I can't… but just know you have fulfilled your promise. Be at peace with that."

"How have I fulfilled my promise? I have never been able to actually be in Diana's presence, near her, in ways that I could interact with her. How have I fulfilled my promise? I was able to dance with her in a dream, but it was only a dream and I could not tell her my feelings. I could not really communicate with her."

"I can't… George said again, his voice trailing off. After a pause, he said, "Find Wily Wizard. He will explain. I feel you are ready to hear an explanation. I'm not the one that can tell you. But know, she loves you. I love you."

And I woke up, lying on my mat.

I thought about the last thing George said. That he loved me. That was strange. But even though I had not found Diana, I didn't feel frustrated anymore. I knew that I needed to find Wily Wizard to ask him what all this meant. I felt at peace, and then I drifted off to sleep.

Part VI

My Promise Fullfilled

The Promise I Made to my Cosmic Companion Fulfilled

Wily Wizard was waiting for me when I next entered the beyond life realm. He was sitting in an open field. I walked up to him and sat beside him on what appeared to be soft grass in the midst of lovely and scented flowers. We sat in silence for a while. I could smell the scent of the wildflowers, and I watched dragonflies and butterflies flying around in the field near us.

Suddenly, Wily Wizard pointed up into the sky—I looked up and saw a vibrant, glowing red streak streaming across the clear blue sky. Then Wily Wizard said, "That's your Diana. She decided she wanted to experience being a fiery comet for a while. She's a feisty one, she is!"

Nothing surprised me anymore, even though I have to admit I first thought to myself, *What? A fiery comet? That's so unlike her—she had so little fire in her natal chart—she was mostly earth and air, with her Sun Sign in Pisces.* But then I reminded myself that she is now truly exploring all sides of herself, her watery sides, her earthy sides, her airy sides, and now her fiery sides—with the essence of that dynamic and amazing comet.

"But I do want you to know that she's satisfied with who she is," Wily Wizard responded, even though I had not said a word. "She is so curious about her other sides, her other essences. Yes, she is intent on exploring, embracing, enjoying, and developing all sides of herself."

Then I felt frustrated again, and said impatiently, "Wait a second, I'm seeing Diana when I catch a glimpse from a distance like this, and then at other times, I am only able to be where she has been and is no longer. Wily Wizard, will I ever be able to ever to just be in the same space with her at the same time and connect with her in a way we can share the experiences that each of us are having in our separate dimensions?"

He did not answer my question directly, but instead said, "You are not just seeing her different expressions of one person as she was on earth, but as separate beings within the essences of her consciousness."

"But when can I find her—who she was or is?"

"She has always been this mixture of beings, her unique blend of multiple beings existing in multiple realities."

"Am I existing now in multiple realities?"

"Yes, you are."

"How come I can't access different sides of myself, like she seems to be doing? That would be weird, but I'd be open to it."

Wily Wizard responded, "You would have a difficult time connecting with your other essences existing in multiple dimensions mainly because your consciousness is still linked to the physical realm of your earth life. But who's to say you haven't already, or one day will be able to run into other sides of yourself."

"That would be weird. What would that be like?"

Wily Wizard said now with his own bit of impatience, "You keep saying the word weird. What does that concept mean, anyway—anything is weird to those people who are not open to the infinite dimensions and possibilities of multiple existences."

Despite seeming irritated, I knew that Wily Wizard was being unusually patient with me, which I really needed at this time. I'd been through so many strange and out of my normal world experiences... I just needed some clarification—actually closure—completion. I needed to connect with Diana or to know why I'm not able to.

Wily Wizard continued, "There's something going on here you need to understand. You have a highly romantic and fiery nature. You've channeled yourself, dedicated yourself to finding whom you call the love of your life—who was a specific being of consciousness that you carry within your soul and is dominating your own consciousness while you are still living in the earth realm. I will admit to you now that even though I initially enabled you to enter into beyond life dimensions, you have been able to continue to come into these beyond life dimensions not just because of me—even though I'm happy to take most of the credit," he smiled and raised his eyebrows, and then continued, "but it's not just me and it's not just you that has allowed you to continue your journeys into these dimensions so easily. You have been able to enter into these dimensions because Diana has been the main entity helping you."

I felt my emotions intensify as he talked. Wily Wizard knew what I was feeling, but continued on, saying something that truly astounded me, "You need to know you have already made contact and interacted with Diana many times. And even though she can't be with you as you knew her in your life on earth, I want you to know that her core essence—and her many essences—are interacting with you the only way she can."

"Please explain to me how that is," I implored.

Wily Wizard continued, "As I have explained, Diana exists in many different multiple dimensions simultaneously. For her to come together and present herself as you knew her, as you want to see and interact with her, is not possible now that she has passed from her life on earth. But she will be waiting for you, and after you have transitioned fully into the afterlife, these various sides of your multi-dimensional essences will be able to connect and intertwine in the most exquisite and lovely ways with your Diana."

"I'm trying to understand what you are saying in my mind, but my heart wants more. Can I at least have the experience of connecting with her even once, even one part of her—in a way that I could communicate more directly with her?"

"You already have—in so many ways..." Wily Wizard responded.

"What do you mean?"

"Many times during your journeys, some of the essences of being you interacted with were actually Diana. I know you hoped that the snake who curled around you in the forest was Diana." I nodded. "That was Diana, as you had hoped. She took a chance there—she shouldn't have done that. The younger woman in Prague who encouraged you to continue your journeys was Diana. So was the young boy in the cistern in Istanbul. She was not only at the river with Henry, but she also was the river you touched with your hand. She was the essence of being who touched you in the art gallery. She was the fencer who led you out of that arena. So she was able to remain distant from you, though connected in the only way she could. Then she started becoming more and more drawn to your presence, and also wanted to interact with you in more complete ways. She began taking too many risks. She was the craft woman at the Country Fair, and as she appeared to you in the heart stone she was actually nearby. When you found yourself in the water-color painting, she was not only the hand that held the paint brush, she was also the canvass that was holding you and even the colors surrounding and caressing you. That was actually Diana who danced with you at the Mediterranean café—it wasn't a dream. And she was George Whitman who told you he loved you."

Then Wily Wizard pointed up to the sky again at the comet that still existed in its fiery form—seemingly both streaking and stationary. "She is sending you her love at this moment as she streaks across this clear blue sky as a fiery red comet."

Wily Wizard continued, "Embrace who she is now. She loves you and has helped you, joined together with you in fulfilling your promise even while you are still living in your earth consciousness."

He then winked at me and said, "Just wait until you do pass. She will be waiting for you, and your existences will be quite dynamic and exhilarating."

"Oh, I hope so. Why are you finally telling me all this now?'

"This is important for you to know. Diana cannot do this any longer. Diana is on her own journeys now and cannot allow herself to be pulled back into the earth realm. If she were to allow herself to connect with you in the way you want, her own essence of being would be compromised. But understand, she will always remain connected with you, her children and grandchildren, her friends in the earth realm, but on her own terms. She has to be completely released by you to explore and integrate all the different sides of her essence. She wanted to have these last opportunities for interacting with you, but she needed to remain distant. She needed you to be unaware that you were actually interacting with her or at least unable to interact with her when you were aware. During your journeys, though, she was becoming too attached to your presence. These last few journeys of yours—at the Country Fair, at the Mediterranean café, in the water color painting, and at the Shakespeare and Company, she was close to presenting herself to you as she was—as you wanted her to remain to be. At the

Oregon Country Fair, after appearing to you in the heart stone she almost allowed you to find her—just as you were always able to find her in the earth realm if the two of you became separated. She almost allowed you to come out of the watercolors painting so the two of you could embrace—she allowed you to see her hand and arm as she painted—she was so close to you. As she danced with you at the Mediterranean café, Diana was too close to crossing the line that would have challenging consequences for her. And then as George Whitman, she almost shifted her appearance into herself as she told you she loved you. She finally realized after those experiences that she could not continue interacting with you. She was losing her own resolve to continue on her own journeys, so we decided to tell you that she would truly be moving on and would not be present any longer, even in the ways she has been. You will be able to continue your journeying into beyond life dimensions through your spiritual imagination if you so choose, but she will not be present in any form or essence any longer while you remain alive in your earth body and consciousness... at least for the foreseeable future...."

I suddenly realized what he had just said, and I interrupted him. "Wait! I thought—you've told me that nobody can see the exact future."

Wily Wizard just smiled briefly. He then continued in the serious manner he had been talking with me before, "As you know there are many possible futures, and we can never tell for sure which ones essences in the physical realms and beyond life dimensions will choose to create for themselves. Now I want to get back to focusing on the future Diana is choosing to create for herself. I hope you will use wisely what I am telling you. Diana will remain connected with you in memories, in dreams, and in your writings while you continue your life on earth. I know you will continue to enjoy her memories and keep the essence of her being in your heart. But she wants you to continue fully living your life on earth as you have been all your life, just as when you met her and entered into a relationship with her. She wants you to continue developing yourself in all ways that you can, and be open to new opportunities for love. She wants you to be happy, and to know that there are really no limits to romantic and intimate love. That's one of the reasons the earth realm exists—to allow beings to experience the physical pleasures and emotional transformations of blending with another person's psyche—and what you call heart.

"You humans are so insecure and tend to encase yourselves in what you see as boundaries of security—fantasies of forever monogamous marriage, rigid religious dos and don'ts, one-track careers, and various sides of the multiple polarities of life. Some of these types of boundary settings are necessary and appropriate at times, but too often they can become barriers to the development of the full potentials that exist beyond these boundaries of security. I do want to acknowledge that more and more of you humans are open to exploring and developing your full potentials beyond these common boundaries you have to function within during your lives in the earth realm. Once you pass, you will experience all of who you are possible of being and all the wisdom you already have within you waiting to be recognized." He stopped and seemed to be a bit concerned. Then he said, "And forget that I used that phrase, *foreseeable future.* You cannot obsess on that. She wants you to create your own future while living, and not to obsess on her any longer."

Wily Wizard put a hand to his head. "I've got to rest a bit now, and you've been here longer than you should be."

I was stunned. I understood what he had told me and felt the joy of Diana's connecting with me. I accepted that I had to let go and continue living my own life without her. Yet I did feel a bit giddy when I thought of the limitless possibilities of *unforeseeable futures.*

Then I could tell Wily Wizard was looking at me sternly, and I quickly responded, "OK, OK, Wily Wizard. Just let me have the full joy of this moment. I promise I won't obsess." Then I realized that he would be going. "Will I see you again?" I asked.

"Oh, for sure! You can't get rid of me now that you've made the leap and made the connection with me. I hope you continue your visits and journeys into these beyond life dimensions. You have developed the ability now without my or Diana's help. You could have many wonderful adventures that will continue to enhance your spiritual imagination and inner peace. And for sure I'll come to visit you from to time to time in your earth realm, especially each year at the Oregon Country Fair—but you may not always recognize me."

"Will you continue to give me guidance?"

"Well sure—but I will also be wanting to tell you my favorite cosmic jokes so that you can continue to laugh at the magical nonsense we all need to enjoy, no matter what dimension or realm we are living in."

I saw twinkles in his eyes. And then the next thing I remember I was waking up on my mat.

As I opened my eyes, I saw a multi-colored silhouette of a figure hovering over me. I knew this was Diana, and she blew me a kiss before she disappeared. I lay on my mat laughing with tears in my eyes. I was feeling so fulfilled as I realized that all this time Diana and I had been interacting and exploring together through the various beyond life dimensions I had visited. We were together, fulfilling a promise to connect with each other, just as we had shared so much in our lives together as one when both of us were living in this earth realm.

Then I was again able to formulate a wish in my consciousness—a wish I wanted to send to the spiritual and lovely essence of being who was, and is, Diana, *"Go where you want and need to go, my love. Fly, fly away with joy on your journeys as you explore and express all of who you are. Thank you for sharing your life with me, both in this earth realm and also in the afterlife dimensions where you are now existing.*

Fly, fly away with joy, my love."

Appendix I

Diana's Art

Diana's Memories of Life in a Catholic Orphanage as a Young child—Art and Writing

A Memory. The day of their arrival at the orphanage, Diana's sister pleads with her mother not to leave; Diana turns to the toy box to discover something of interest in the new environment.

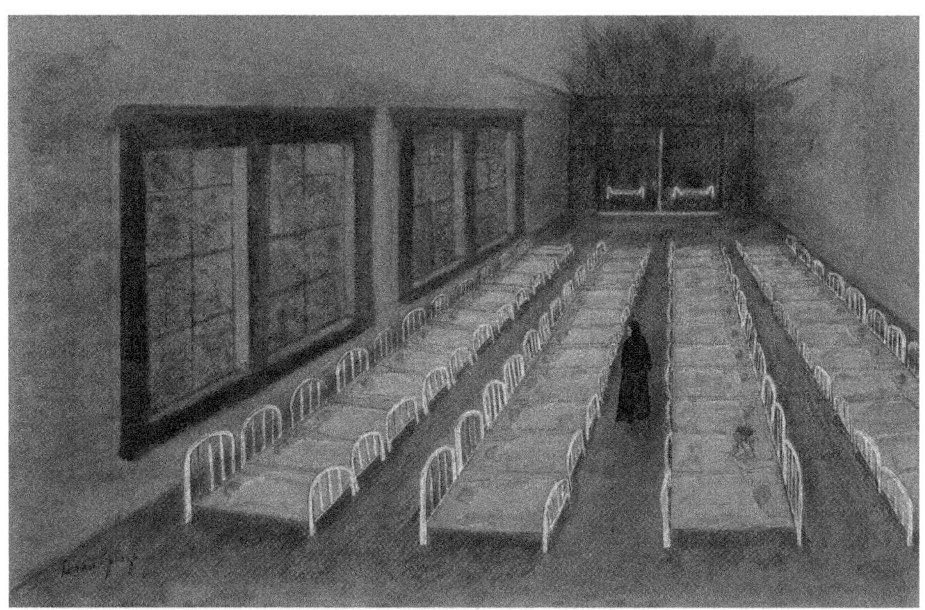

Diana and other children try to comfort a younger child who is afraid of Father Christmas.

THE NIGHT WE LEFT THE ORPHANAGE, I WAS GIVEN A DOLL TO TAKE HOME. IT ~~WAS SURPRISED~~ ~~AND~~ WASN'T EASY AT FIRST TO GRASP THIS — BECAUSE ALL THE TOYS BELONGED TO EVERYONE.

AS I SEE IT NOW — I'M SURE THE SISTER NOTICED I ALWAYS CHOSE THIS DOLL AND THAT I WAS VERY ATTACHED TO IT. THIS DOLL WAS THE FIRST OF 12 I ACCRUED DURING MY YEARS AFTER I LEFT THE ORPHANAGE. THEY ALL SLEPT TOGETHER IN THE SAME DOLL CRIB AND EACH WAS GIVEN A NAME TO SUIT HER INDIVIDUALITY.

THIS DOLL WITH THE QUITE LARGE PIECE MISSING FROM HER HEAD, HIDDEN BY THE BEAUTIFUL BABY CAP SHE WORE, WAS AS REAL TO ME THEN AS A BABY CAN BE, TO ANYONE WHO LOVES IT. YEARS LATER MOTHERING MY LITTLE BABIES I FELT THE SAME COMPASSION AND LOVE AS I TOUCHED THEIR TOES OR FINGERS AND REALIZED THE SUPREME FAITH I WAS TRUSTED WITH BY THESE TINY OLD SOULS.

Leaving the Orphanage with a Doll—Tiny Old Souls

Diana's Paintings and Drawings of Her Dreams

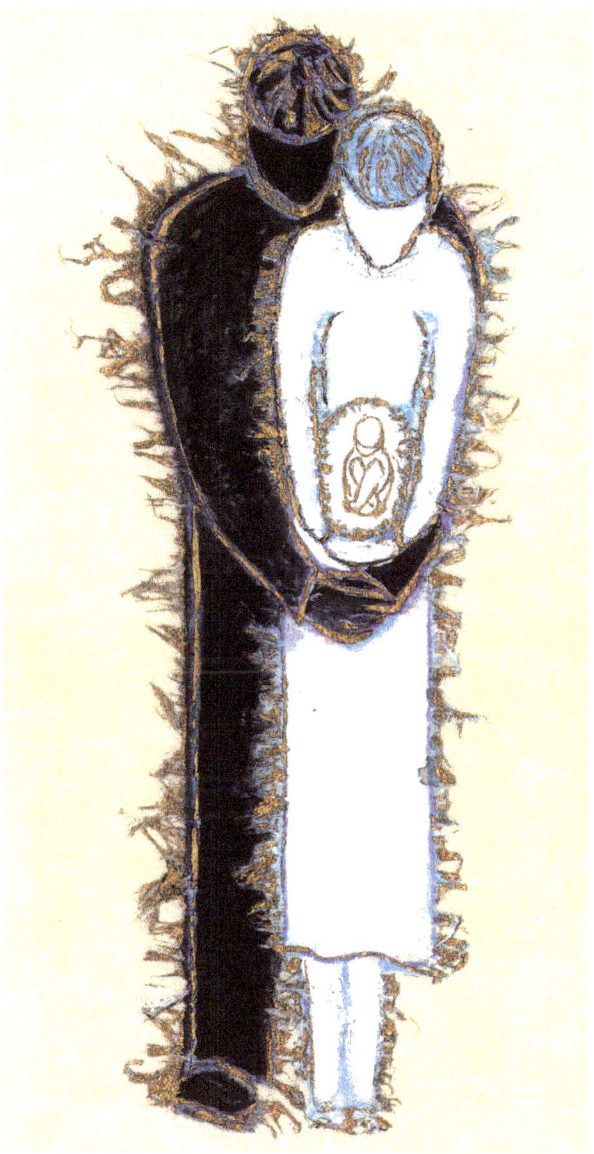

A Collage. A dark male (tinged in many colors), a white woman (tinged in many colors), and a child in utero (tinged in gold and held in the three-circled, egg-shaped embrace of male, female, and the sheltering womb symbolize the potential birth of a Divine Child.

Diana offers food to Cambodian refugees traveling by boat in underground caves. A man carries those who are injured to dry land so that she may feed them, allow them to rest, and heal their injuries.

Diana is cooking and serving food in her treasured new house, a Gothic cathedral. Her kitchen is located in front of an intricately carved alter covered with ice crystals.

Paris Art

Paris Park

Paris park in oil

Structure in Paris

Paris café

Woman on street in Paris

Paris guesthouse stairway

Man with red scarf in Paris

Diana's Other Art Expressions

Hug from above

Hug from above #2

Sketches of children (from left clockwise: Tracy, Katy, Madeline, Alicia and James drinking a glass of water)

Diana's sculpture of a Gargoyle on one of our inner courtyard walls

Woman in gold

Self-photograph

Diana took these last two photographs with a 35mm camera on a tripod. Her right arm was holding the switch connected to a cable which was connected to the camera. I suppose these photographs could be considered old-school selfies. I've always loved the lighting and this moment of sharing captured in this last photograph.

Appendix II

Music

Recommended Music to Enhance Your Reading Experience

I.   Any of the music from the albums of **Omar Akram**, an Afghani-American musician, but specifically the following songs:

From the album *Free As A Bird:* "Free As A Bird," "Surrender," "A Passage to Midnight," "Dancing in the Wind," "Beauty Unveiled," "Never Let Go."

From the album *Echoes of Love:* "Echoes of Love," "Lovely Day," "Draw Me Close," "My Hope Is You," "Free Spirit."

From the album *Secret Journey:* "Secret Journey," "Passage of the Night," "Shimmering Star," "Angel of Hope," "Mirage," "Gypsy Spirit."

II.   Any of the music from the albums of Mediterranean guitarist, **Priyo**, but specifically the following songs:

From the album *Gypsy Lullaby:* "Spazio," "Caramba," "Assaibene," "Ocean," "Fotuna," " Carrettero."

From the album *Gypsy Grooves:* "Mio Amor," "Mars Walk," "Emauela," "Raggi Caldi," "Djembe Spirit."

From the album *Gypsy Moon:* "Canzone Latina," "Dolcezza," "Gypsy Trance," "Cool Passion."

III.   Any of the music from the albums of **Andrea Bocelli**, but specifically the following songs:

From the album *Amore:* "Amapola," "Besame Mucho," "Canzoni Stonato," "Cuando Me Enamoro," "L'Appuntamento (Senstado a 'beira do caminho)."

IV.   Any of the music from the albums of **Luciana Pavarotti.**

V.   Any of the music from the albums of **Pink Martini,** but specifically the following songs:

From the album *Hey Eugene:* "Everywhere," "Tempo Perdido," "Mar Desconocido," "City of Night," Taya Tan," "Ojala," "Cante E Dance."

VI.   Any of the music from the albums of the Corsican band, **I Muvrini,** but specifically the following songs:

From the album *I Muvrini:* "Ne Fermez Pas La Porte," "A Morte Di Filicone," "Curagiu," "Un Mi Ne Di Piu," "Terra."

From the album *Alma:* "Alma," "Per Amore," "Turneranu qui," "Era Una Volta," "Le Temps Qu'il Fera."

From the album *Gioa:* "Una Terranova," "Elli A Sanu," Gioa," "O Corsica Tu," "Ti Dicu Di Tu."

VII.   Any of the music from the albums of Brazilian singer, **Marisa Monte,** but specifically the following songs:

From the album *Live from Sao Paulo:* "Depois (Au Vivo," "Ilusao (Illusion) (featuring Julieta Venegas)," "O Que Se Quer."

From the album O Que Voce Quer Saber de Verdade: "Lencinho Querido (El Panuelito)," "Aquela Velha Cancao," "Verdade Uma Busao," "Bem Aqui."

VIII.   Any of the music from the album *Azure,* from **Mediterranean Nights,** but specifically the following songs: "Cyprus Sunset," "A La Vida," "Iris," "Nights On The Mediterranean," "Echoes of the East," "Unrequited Love."

IX. Any of the following specific songs from the following singers:

"My Sweet Lord," "Wah, Wah," "Isn't It a Pity," "All Things Must Pass," "Inner Light" by **George Harrison;** "Imagine," "Starting Over," "Jealous Guy," "Woman" by **John Lennon;** "A La Vida," by Edith Piaf; "Heaven" by **Joe Cocker;** "Layla" by Eric Clapton.

Playlist for Diana's Celebration of Life–Before the Ceremony

1. **Assaibene** (*Priyo*)
2. **Sei Viva** (*Priyo*)
3. **Pero Te Extano** (*Andrea Bocelli*)
4. **A Morte Di Filicone** (*I Muvrini*)
5. **Al Sheraa Al Maksour** (*Omat Khairat*)
6. **Chileno** (*Priyo*)
7. **Canzone Latina** (*Priyo*)
8. **La Donna Cannone** (*Francesco de Gregori*)

Playlist for Diana's Celebration of Life– After the Ceremony

1. **My Sweet Lord** (*George Harrison*)
2. **La Donna Cannone** (*Francesco de Gregori*)
3. **La Soledad** (*Pink Martini*)
4. **Layla** (*Eric Clapton*)
5. **Chileno** (*Priyo*)
6 **Curagiu** (*I Muvrini*)
7. **Aspettami** (*Pink Martini*)
8. **Al Sheraa Al Maksour** (*Omar Khairat*)
9. **Love** (*John Lennon*)
10. **Hear Me Lord** (*George Harrison*)
11. **Unchained Melody** (*The Righteous Brothers*)
12. **Everywhere** (*Pink Martini*)
13. **Your Warm and Tender Love** (*Chris Rea*)
14. **Harvest Moon** (*Neil Young*)
15. **Sway** (*Pink Martini*)
16. **Shine On You Crazy Diamond** (*Pink Floyd*)

Appendix III

Special Appreciations!

Special Appreciations of Family and Friends in This Earth Realm and Beyond

As I come to the end of describing my journeys through caregiving, grieving and entering into beyond life dimensions to find and reconnect with my life-love partner—I have been reflecting on all the family and friends who have been a loving, supportive and sustaining part of our lives. I want to express my deepest appreciation to the following people. I realize that there are many more people whom we've been close to and interacted in meaningful ways than I have listed below, and I hope you know that you are also in our hearts and souls.

I want to express my love and appreciation to all of our children and grandchildren for being so present and supportive of both Diana and I during the 5 years of their mother and Oma's life. They visited often and sent videos and photographs and gave Diana so much joy as she progressed through her illness. I want to especially acknowledge Tracy and Marc Murfitt for their consistent caregiving presence and support during Diana's illness. They moved to Eugene into our house when Diana was diagnosed with Alzheimer's, and were present at some part of every day to help me, as well as the caregivers, provide Diana what she needed. Marc had a job where he could work at home, and Marc spent so much quality time with Diana. They had a lively and fun time together.

When Diana first became diagnosed with her condition, the house next door in our Tiara Street Community came up for sale. I was fortunate enough to find a way to purchase this house with our daughter, Katy, so that she and one of our other daughter's, Alicia, could live there and be near their mother. I want to thank Anita Stelling, one of the original Tiara Community members, who provided special support that enabled me to purchase this house. Mae Klein and Craig Timmons also provided supportive information and encouragement, and I also want to thank the owner of the house, Betsy Ruth, who was very accommodating as we finalized this purchase. Katy and her daughter, Iris, moved into one section of the house next door, and Alicia moved into the other section. Their presence gave Diana and I so much comfort having them so close throughout Diana's illness. Alicia is a Doctor of Chinese Medicine and an Acupuncturist, who has always provided the family with healing care and whose interventions gave her mom sustaining and healthy comfort. Madeline Derby McKee who lived in Portland visited often and sent videos, and James and Jodi Derby, who lived in Indiana, also remained in continual contact through calls and videos of the family. I want to acknowledge my son and his wife, David and Jill Mann. David stayed in touch each week, and our sharing was both enjoyable and encouraging. Diana's brother, Michael Armendariz, who was visiting his grown son in Eugene, came over every Sunday and shared brunch with us, and Diana enjoyed his presence

I want to thank all the grandchildren, now ages 10 to

29: Whitney Pitman, Sofia Murfitt, Remy Murfitt, Wyatt Keuter, Lexi Pitman, Jasmine Keuter, Iris Keuter, Bella McKee, Ethan Derby, Ava Derby, Monica Derby and Jackson Derby. Henry McKee passed away in March, 2019 at age 14, and had a special connection with his Oma.

I want to express my appreciation to the children's father, Jim Derby and his wife Amy. Diana and Jim remained friends after they divorced, and we often shared family gatherings together over the years. They were supportive of both of us during her illness, and we would meet with them at a café or pub once a week for brief visits. Diana enjoyed these visits so much.

Diana's mother, Marie Armendariz, who was born in San Marcos, Nicaragua, passed away in 1998 at the age of eighty-three. Marie became a single mother of five children in the late 1940s, when very few social services and support options. She decided to place her children in a Catholic orphanage run by mostly German nuns so that she could find work that would eventually enable her to bring her children home. She worked her way up into higher paying positions, and as soon as she could, she brought her children home. Diana often talked about her mother's strength, love and sacrifices that enabled her to provide for the family, while also creating a nurturing environment with proper discipline. Since her mother worked, Diana and her siblings each had chores to do, and Diana continued this practice as she raised her own children.

I want to also acknowledge my mother, June Farrar. My mother was a Southern, somewhat conventional, woman who had an open and loving nature. I have to admit I wondered how she would react to my falling in love and deciding to live with a woman who had five young children, yet she embraced and fell in love with Diana, our children and eventually our grandchildren. As my mother's health declined during the last year of her life, the children took turns living in the house to help care for her. My mother died on Mother's day, 1999, and all the children and grandchildren who had been born were present in the house in Eugene celebrating Mother's Day. It was a loving passing.

My older brother, John Mann, his wife Ruby, and their family live in Canada. My younger brother, Mike Farrar and his wife Jill and their family live in Texas. For most of our adult lives we've generally lived about as far away from each other on the North American continent as possible. Yet we have remained close and interactive across the distances, and our relationships through the years have been emotionally important to both Diana and I, and especially as we've journeyed through the experience of Diana's passing.

I want to specifically acknowledge our long-term friend, Sylvia Weisshaupt, a Jungian Psychologist. We met Sylvia in 1976 about the time Diana and I started living together. Then in the early 1980s, Diana chose to do analytical work with Sylvia in order to become more conscious of her psychological-spiritual essence and potentials. Sylvia used some of her dreams as part of her Jungian thesis. In 1985 Sylvia invited Diana to attend the Jungian Summer Program in Küsnacht, Switzerland with her for a summer session. See Appendix I for samples of Diana's paintings based upon her dream work. Sylvia has been a close friend and mentor during all 41 years Diana and I have been together. She is a wise and vibrant woman in her early 90's, and is still providing consulting and group work guidance to others.

I want to thank Diana's close friends, Dieter and Edeltraut Nerlich, who live in Northern Germany near the Denmark border. We would Skype every week. Diana met Dieter and Edeltraut in 1971 and remained close with their family ever since. In 2014, I was able to arrange a trip for Diana to see Dieter and Edeltraut and our other German friends one last time while she was still functioning well enough to travel. She was able to provide herself general self-care, but she still needed special attention and could not be left alone in public or she would have gotten lost. Our German friends were so caring and generous and I know that Diana felt happy and satisfied even though she did not know it would be the last time she would be seeing them. I want to additionally acknowledge, Ben Warkentin and his wife and family, Sepp Mayerhafer, Walter and Karin Mayerhafer and their family, Gerhard Graf, Martin and Finsterwald and his family, Marc Nerlich, Sabina Nerlich and Sven and their children, Lena, Layla, and Louis. I want to express my appreciation to Brigitte Gueyraud, an artist and art therapist who lives in Paris, and who became friends with Diana when she lived in the city for three months in 1995. I want to thank Erin and Gabrielle Nozoglia who let us stay with them in Santa Margherita Ligure, Italy in 2011, and Aroon Khalsi and Sofia Mancini who arranged a house exchange for us at Sofia's parent's olive farm in Fiesole, Italy that same summer.

I want to acknowledge Jin Kim Hurfeld, who lived in our house for a brief time when she visited Eugene as part of a student exchange in the early 1990s. She has remained a close friend during all of these years. I want to acknowledge Poppi, whose Greek and Italian restaurant (Poppi's Anatolia) has been Diana and my favorite over the years, and Poppi's sister, Stella Mantheakis and her daughter Louanna. Stella has been a "larger than life" person in our lives. She invited us to Greece and entertained us there on two wonderful occasions.

I want to acknowledge our Tiara Street neighbors whose presence also provided both Diana and I sustained comfort. In 1995, Diana and I read a mission statement written by the founders of the Tiara Neighborhood Community, which emphasized the values of community sharing and ecological house building. We met with one of the initial members of the community, Hannah Still, and instantly knew we wanted to purchase and try to build a house so that we could be a part of this community. Hannah passed away in 2012 at age 87, but her vision and essence has remained a central part of this community over the years. I want to acknowledge Debbie Olsen and her family, Annie Brown, Twyla

Jacobosen and Mike Barnes, Jerry Brule and Cherie Black, Neal and Marta Spangler, Leila Snow, Arun Toke and Bidyut Das, Carol Goodman, Beckie Borchardt, Marleen Marshall, Sue Schumacher and Lloyd Hamilton and many others in the neighbor who provided such loving support.

I especially want to thank so many other friends whose visits lifted Diana's spirits throughout the last years of her life: Antonia Putzi Esmario, Karen Tyler, LaHoma Simmons, Lisa Wagner (who has passed), Elisabeth Warkentin (who has also passed), Rachel Vail and Michael Schwartz. I want to acknowledge Diana's social work friends, Kim Davidson, Kathy Kroeger and Georgene Ollerenshaw, who spent two years studying closely together in their cohort group at Portland State University as they completed their Master's Degree in Social Work.

I want express appreciation for astrologer colleagues who have been close friends to both Diana and I, and whom we have enjoyed and gained meaningful insights during our many gatherings over the years. I want to specifically acknowledge Claudia Lapp and Gary Rabideau, who kept the astrological salon meetings in Eugene going, which provided astrologers and astrology students a forum to learn, discuss and enhance their skills. I also want to honor astrologers, tarot readers and psychics, Johanna Mitchell and Connie Bender both of whom passed within a few months of each other (Johanna in December, 2018 and Connie in February,

2019 (after attending Johanna's Celebration of Life ceremony). Both of these wise and expressive spiritual guides provided such joy and meaningful metaphysical insights for our family over the years, as they did to so many other people.

I want to thank Robert Gulley, Jack Trachsel, Jaye Stutz and Doug Hoss for being such close and supportive friends.

I was so fortunate to have wonderful and skilled care-givers including Kathleen Meyers-welch, Joan Martin, Ginger Gietzen and Lillian Ames. Our granddaughter, Iris Keuter, provided caregiving services off and on during the whole five years of Diana's illness. She went with us to the Saturday Market every week and to every Oregon Country Fair with us during the past few years. Her help was not only invaluable, but also special that she was able and wanted to share these experiences with us. Diana and I have always felt blessed to have the loving and caring family and friends that we had in our lives.

I feel fortunate to have been enhanced by Diana and her children and their grandchildren with the spirit of love and diversity. I am so appreciative to have been a part of the life of Diana Zelaya and our family and friends throughout the world and in beyond life dimensions.